Witch's Bones

Copyright © 2022 Tommy L Barton
All rights reserved.

All rights reserved. This book, or parts, may not be reproduced in any form without permission from the author.

ISBN

Witch's Bones

By Tommy L Barton

Thanks

Table of Contents

Chapter One 1

Chapter Two 10

Chapter Three 14

Chapter Four 21

Chapter Five 24

Chapter Six 31

Chapter Seven 40

Chapter Eight 43

Chapter Nine 49

Chapter Ten 54

Chapter Eleven 59

Chapter Twelve 62

Chapter Thirteen 65

Chapter Fourteen 67

Chapter Fifteen 70

Chapter Sixteen 74

Chapter Seventeen 79

Chapter Eighteen 86

Chapter Nineteen 89

Chapter Twenty 94

Chapter Twenty-One 98

Chapter Twenty-Two 100

Chapter Twenty-Three 104

Chapter Twenty-Four 108

Chapter Twenty-Five 112
Chapter Twenty-Six 116
Chapter Twenty-Seven 118
Chapter Twenty-Eight 121
Chapter Twenty-Nine 124
Chapter Thirty 126
Chapter Thirty-One 129
Chapter Thirty-Two 134
Chapter Thirty-Three 137
Chapter Thirty-Four 142

Chapter One

Sandra Laughlin sat at her counter, flipping pages in a magazine. Her face shined from the sweat. Her blonde eyebrows acted as a dam, stopping the saline drops from stinging her crystal blue eyes. She absently rubbed the bridge of her Grecian nose to stop the slight itching of the salt. She licked her full lips unconsciously to keep them moist in the heat. Her long blonde hair felt heavy from being damp. Pearls and streaks of sweat gathered at her voluptuous cleavage exposed by a skimpy red camisole. The red cotton fabric clung to her flat belly, accentuating her curvy hips. She wore a white pair of capri pants in a vain attempt to beat the stifling heat. Consequently, from sitting on the wooden stool, the moisture gathered around her thighs and below her buttocks. Her petite feet, clad in dollar store flip flops, braced her legs on the bottom rung of the stool. She glanced at the open door to her bookstore hoping for a breeze in the sultry heat of a summer afternoon in South Carolina. Only the bravest souls endured the hazy, late afternoon heat. Sandra cursed her luck that the air conditioner had broken down for the third time this summer.

Boundless Books was the name of Sandra's store, an amalgamation of books, incense, candles, and the odd tribal masks. End caps displayed the latest pulp fiction and an eclectic collection of books leaned on shelves. Little alcoves harbored unassuming figurines to the untrained eye. Usually, an incense burner spewed sandalwood into the air, but Sandra didn't want to add to the heat. A metal spiral stair case in the corner of the store led to a spacious apartment upstairs. At the moment the private apartment gathered the rising heat of the day. The store front let in the sun's rays; plate glass windows making a luminous wall. No decoration adorned the windows but the name Boundless Books was emblazoned with white paint on the black awning above and outside the door frame. The only intrusive fixtures were two glass shelves half-way up on each side of the door. The penetrable store front windows were like a huge showcase showing the shelves and the shop beyond. Each shelf sparkled in the sun from its contents. On the left, geodes and crystal bowls full of natural stones such as amethyst, cat's eye, river stones, and other odd assortments. On the right, velvet cases held silver jewelry. Ankhs, stars, and other odd patterns hung as pendants on light silver chains. The store, clean and neat, harbored Sandra's hopes and dreams.

Sandra's store rested in a niche of other store-fronts in the middle of an old downtown area of the town Clear View. Located in the heart of South Carolina, Clear View remained small for a town located only twenty miles from Columbia, the capitol of South Carolina. The locals had fought to keep out national chains of restaurants, retailers, and drug stores. Being only miles from the capitol, Clear View townies wanted to remain small and unobtrusive. Besides, anything could be bought in Columbia if a townie decided to make the thirty-minute trip down Interstate 20 to the capitol. The downtown area harbored all the shops for Clear View. A local drug store, men's apparel, lady's apparel, butcher, and other stores catered to the locals. Sometime in the middle of the twentieth century; the only new construction allowed downtown in living memory, the mayor's son of the time built a single auditorium for a movie theater. Peevishly, the old timers lamented on the new construction. Today, the theater shined like a beacon at the end of the street with its marquee, and Sandra's store, located only three store fronts down from the theater, enjoyed the after-hour crowds of twenty something's and teenagers.

Sandra imagined she felt a cool breeze on the back of her neck from the register in the ceiling above the counter. Jim, the local handyman, strolled into the shop from the back store room that led out into a back alley of the street. Sandra turned and said, "I thought you would never finish."

Jim set a metal tool box on the counter and said, "It's only temporary. You need a new unit." He pulled a handkerchief from the front pocket of the jean overalls he had worn every day for the past thirty years. His wife had bought him a new set of six overalls for Christmas last year. He bought her a French Maid outfit in Columbia. There was something to be said about discretion in a small town. He dabbed the side of his neck and said, "They don't make them anymore with the old

Freon. You're going to have to call McCafflin if you want it fixed again."

"Why the old horse trader act, Jim?" asked Sandra. "You've been working on my coolant for years."

"Well, now, you need a license to buy the old Freon coolant now. McCafflin has a business license, so he'll have to work on it for now on," said Jim. "So don't give me that pouting face."

Sandra stopped being facetious with her face, and replied, "Well, I guess I'll just have to steal a bottle from McCafflin next time."

Jim sighed, and his face turned serious.

"Sandra, can I speak to you for a moment?" he asked.

Sandra looked at Jim quizzically, and said, "Sure, if you need to, but go shut the door, the airs going out."

Jim kicked the door jamb out from the corner of the glass door. It slowly swung shut, making a loud clanking noise before resting home. Above the door, an old cow bell hung on a rod over the door acted as an announcement for the store.

"What are you fretting about, old man," said Sandra half joking.

Walking back to the counter, Jim replied, "It's about Marla."

Marla, Jim's nineteen-year-old daughter, had been a surprise for Jim and his wife Rebecca. Both of them had been in their thirties when Marla, born in Clear View by a prostitute from Columbia, had been quietly given to the couple from the old country doctor who treated her mother after the birth and knew how much Jim and Rebecca wanted a child. Very few people knew about the illegal adoption, but Sandra was one of the few.

"We think she's pregnant, and the damn boy has run off," said Jim hotly.

"Have you asked her?" replied Sandra coolly.

Jim stopped, and said quietly, "We have asked her, but all she does is stay in her room and cry all day. I mean, I just want to help her one way or another. I just can't fix it if I don't know the problem." The old man looked absolutely abject in his misery.

"Knowing the answer might be worse." When Jim began to protest, Sandra held up a hand and said, "I'll help." Jim was a dear friend of Sandra's. She felt obligated to help; not only for his sake, but also for the nineteen-year-old and obviously distressed Marla. "Lock the door and come up to the apartment," Sandra said. She dropped down from her perch and moved up the stairs.

Jim had been in Sandra's apartment on several occasions. On Sandra's twenty-first birthday he had actually brought her safely home and tucked her into bed. The apartment; sparsely furnished to give it an open feeling, had been in Sandra's family for several generations. Usually, the apartment had been set aside for the manager of the family produce store, but Sandra had renovated the bottom into a bookstore. Being the only survivor of an agrarian family, Sandra had sold the family house and rapidly shrinking plot of farming land to pay for her parent's debts. Jim sat on the couch and waited patiently for Sandra to come out of the only room he had never been in before. He instinctively knew that the room concealed Sandra's sanctuary. The room had no door; only a tapestry of gold thread and intricate purple patterns, split down the middle with the edges sewn by Sandra to cover the doorway. Jim ducked his head as Sandra parted the tapestry and stepped into the living room of the apartment.

"Is that a toy?" asked Jim, trying to keep his tone casual. The palms of his hands were sweating profusely, but not from the heat. He felt like he needed a drink of water because his mouth was suddenly so dry. He was rethinking about asking Sandra for help. Jim had never asked Sandra to perform magic for him. He felt scared, and a little intimidated by the slightly over a hundred-pound woman.

Sandra sat down in a lotus position across from Jim in front of the coffee table. She placed a white sheet of paper on the table. Then, she placed a heart shaped, dark wooden planchette in the middle of the piece of printer paper. The planchette had two green vines originating from the bottom to curve around the heart shaped top with two white roses at the end of the vines almost touching in the middle of the planchette. On the bottom of the planchette, two caster wheels were secured to the back half, and a clasp held a pencil on the tip forming a wheelbase tripod.

Sandra rested both her pointer fingers on the heart shaped top. She smiled up at Jim and replied, "In a way, you can think of this as a toy. It belonged to my great grandmother. Now, take three deep breaths and close your eyes," She waited for Jim to comply before saying, "Try to look at the back of your eyelids, empty your mind, and relax. Open your eyes and place your pointer finger on the tip of the planchette behind the pencil. Now ask yourself three times if your daughter is pregnant and remove your finger."

Jim and Sandra removed their fingers at the same time. Nothing happened for a moment and Jim exhaled a deep breath. He caught his breath on the inhale, and could not breathe for a second as he watched the planchette slowly write a word on the crisp white paper with the lead pencil.

Jim stared at Sandra, and whispered, "What does it say? I don't have my glasses on."

Sandra looked up at Jim, and smiled. "It spelled the word "yes," you're going to be a grandfather."

Jim leaned back onto the couch and then laughed openly. "I'm going to be a grandfather. Oh mother, I am going to be a grandfather," repeated Jim.

A loud clanging noise rose from the stairs. "Did you lock the shop door Jim?" asked Sandra as she stood up and headed for the top of the stairs.

"No, child, I just shut it." Jim stood up quickly with a huge grin on his face. "I have to get home and speak to my daughter."

As Sandra headed down the stairs, she called back, "Don't forget the paper. It's yours."

In the rush to get out, Jim grabbed the paper and crumpled it up as he put it in his pocket. If he had taken time to notice, he would have read the second word on the paper. In bold cursive, the word spelled DANGER.

***

Clear View as a town had slowly progressed into the twenty-first century like a caterpillar slowly progresses into a butterfly. The local college had resolutely kept Clear View progressive; even if the town did not wish to transform itself into something modern. Living in such a small southern town, the young Indonesian woman routinely found herself blithely ignoring the stares of its citizens. To her perception, it was not apparent whether those staring found her incredibly beautiful or were just offended at her brown skin even though it was the twenty-first century.

Ida Makmur, a third generation American, always took the initiative and introduced herself first. No one usually asked her how to spell her last name, since asking would be too embarrassing for both Ida and the other person. She never seemed to come to rest, including exercising a frolicsome and sometimes sharp tongue. Ida seemed to be as endearingly bright internally as she was physically dark. Her bright smile captured her intense love of life. Her long black hair, dark eyes, and brown skin exuded a dark sultriness. She wore a peach, strapless, paisley print dress that contrasted with her dark-skinned curves. Like any other day, she was walking with a chipper step down the sidewalk of Clear View's downtown street. She was on her way to Sandra's bookstore, a way she could walk blindfolded, and so her mind faded in and out of reminiscence.

Ida had wanted to go to college since the first day of high school. Her family only conceded when Ida explained how a woman could only find a suitable husband in a college setting. She wanted to study to be a lawyer, but her family thought legalities did not suit a young woman. Finally, after considerable thought, she settled on studying library administration. At least then she could exercise her tongue by choosing the appropriate book someone would need. Ida never did find a suitable mate at her alma mater; much to the disappointment of her parents. Ida did find a different path.

Stopping at a crosswalk, waiting for the light, Ida thought about her college life. Ida's collegiate studies at Brooksforth College were in stark contrast to her social endeavors. The girls disdained Ida, probably because she was direct competition for appropriating a suitable husband from the law school in the nearby town. The only small consolation for Ida was the drama department. The drama boys and girls expressed a freedom incomprehensible to the uptight gold mongers of the student body at Brooksforth College. Ida never felt attracted to the drama boys due to their immaturity. She did have clandestine affairs with a couple of graduate teachers' assistants and one college professor. The introductory college courses, Ida found, were ill conceived and contrite; not really making a dent in her day-to-day life, but a tome she found in the basement of the library the first week of classes would forever shape the course of her life.

The annals described the persecution of witches throughout history, including the grotesque Salem witch trials. The tome intrigued Ida. She had felt persecuted since the first day of high school. The pubescent teens had ridiculed and humiliated her for being Indonesian. Ida had convinced herself that college would be different. College was a learning experience; especially when the classes focused on library administration, but things were not much different than high school. Other girls still ridiculed her and she couldn't convince herself the taunting came from inherent jealousy. Perhaps if she had she would have felt more confident about herself. The freedom and the balance of nature inherent in the Wiccan faith contrasted with Ida's sense of constriction instituted by her parents and classmates. She longed for truly uninhibited freedom of sexuality and unconventional thought. The thespians embraced her with unconditional support for her journey of self-discovery. The theater alumni taught her freedom of expression of both the mind and the body. Wicca taught her balance.

Passing a couple of store fronts, her mind drifted to post college. After four years of college and practicing Wicca, Ida landed a job as a library director. Even in a small town, the library director made more money than the average American. The library scooped her up after college and paid her less than a more prestigious library would have but didn't require more than her bachelor's degree. It was a great opportunity for a recent college graduate. After working a year in the library, Ida thought she had made the wrong decision as the small town seemed to strangle her. Then she met Sandra. Sandra was like fresh water in a desert. Both of them clicked together like Legos. Their friendship blossomed into a sisterhood.

Sandra introduced her to a familial coven of witches. As a solitary practitioner for the last five years, Ida felt relief and joy at finding like-minded people in the seemingly backwater environs of a small southern town. Ida was to be an acolyte for the next couple of years before she was fully assimilated into the coven. During her second spring equinox ritual with the coven her initiation had been completed.

As the last, thirteenth member to join the coven, she had been given the moniker Mocking Bird.

A year later, an anniversary as she understood it, Ida considered the vernal sabbat a form of rebirthing. Ida had been prepared over the last couple of years by the coven to strengthen her feelings of communion instead of continuing to follow her solitary pursuits as a witch.

Ida's thoughts swirled as she thought about that glorious night sabbat. Consumed by her thoughts, she walked as if in a trance down the unimpeded sidewalk. Imagining facing a pyre of burning wood in one of the coven's member's cow pastures, Ida remembered her naked front embraced in the fires warmth while her buttocks felt the chill night air. An homage to abundance and resurrection to the coven, the ritual targeted Serapis, a lower world Greek god. If only the coven knew something else listened to the night wind.

That night, Ida felt like a coiled spring. As the ritual progressed, her vision narrowed in to focus on the fire. The coven surrounding the fire worked a blessing from Serapis. In response to their impassioned liturgy, the coven was inundated with sexual energy. Ida became a creature of sensations long forgotten. How it felt to be a virgin, even though she had forgotten the coursing blood and feeling of electricity on her skin. She felt flushed, out of breath. She felt ashamed of her fervency at seeing nudity, which drove her lust. Her skin crawled with static electricity while being touched. Her heart hammered in her chest as she felt her hands touch others' loins. Her muscles shook as men and women caressed her. She abandoned her mediocrity to embrace the divine while coalescing with the coven. The night culminated with her on her back looking up at the stars. She felt like she lived a thousand years in just one moment as tears escaped her wonderous eyes.

Coming out of her seeming trance, she smiled at a passerby feeling naturally wholesome. The young man stumbled as he passed her trying to see more than her smile. She took no notice of the boy, instead she thought of the spell after the ritual. The blessing from Serapis had incorporated her into the communal powers of the coven. A simple spell, she created a natural compass of a leaf in a copper bowl of water; the stem always pointing due north as she walked around her apartment. Never before had a spell felt so natural and uninhibited.

"Goober peas, ma'am?" asked a vendor on the street. The man had completely broken Ida's reverie.

"I'm sorry, what?" asked Ida confusedly.

"Don't bother, Jake. That brown girl doesn't know what southern boiled peanuts are," said a heavy-set woman in a store front's doorway. The woman's friend, a skinny young girl, giggled and buried her head into the woman's shoulder.

Ida glanced at the peanut cart. A silver box with a red umbrella, it looked endemic to the town. She replied to Jake, looking directly at the women, "She's right, I never know what kind of nuts I will find in the south." She nodded to Jake before moving on down the street.

They stared at the back of Ida's head until she cleared the next intersection.

Chapter Two

The night before the grisly murder, Anita Lark sat in her usual place at the end of the bar. The bar's name was Hanky Pinky and it was girl's night. The bar, located on the outskirts of Columbia, South Carolina, catered to lesbians on Thursday nights. One night a week, Anita felt like she was in her element. People in Clear View treated Anita with respect but never engaged with her. Anita owned a men's clothing store "The Haberdashery" in downtown Clear View. All the goods were imported from London, England. Men's silk ties, French cuff shirts, vests, and an assortment of sundry things could be found at the store.

Right now, Anita wore a new men's vest she sold at her shop. Men's clothes fit Anita well because of her slender build. Also, Anita felt good because her favorite bartender gave her a positive comment about the green vest and her latest hair style. Anita had decided to cut her brown hair. Now she sported a pageboy haircut.

The bar was bouncing tonight. A D.J. pumped out music. Girls danced on the elevated stage in the middle of the bar. You had to be careful not to fall off while dancing. The stage stood a foot higher than the floor. Waitresses meandered through the crowd taking drink orders at small tables around the dance floor. Anita saw a woman walk out of the crowd towards her. Anita's heart beat a little faster. She had never seen such fiery red hair. Anita locked eyes with her trying to get her attention. The girl smiled at Anita and strolled up to the bar.

"Is this seat taken?" asked the girl. The girl was dressed provocatively. She wore a blouse with no sleeves. Cutoff jeans at the boundaries of her ass with fish net stockings covering her long legs tucked into her black boots.

"No, have at it," answered Anita. "Can I buy you a drink?"

"A gin and tonic," replied the girl. "My name is Myra. What's yours?"

"Anita." Waving down a bartender, she said, "Ben, can I get a gin and tonic for the lady."

"Anita. Sounds Irish," said Myra.

Anita laughed, "I don't know about that."

"So, Anita. Why the men's vest?" asked Myra as she accepted the drink from the bartender.

"You don't like it?" asked Anita with concern in her voice.

"I find it interesting."

"I own a men's clothing store. I like to wear a piece every time I come here."

"Ballsy for fashion, but it is the eighties," said Myra smiling over her drink.

"And fish net stockings are in?" asked Anita coyly.

"Maybe, maybe not, but I like the style."

"I think it looks great on you."

"I would like to see them on your bedroom floor."

Anita laughed, "Maybe after a couple more drinks."

Myra held up her glass, and said, "Cheers."

Anita clinked her glass against Myra's glass, and said, "To an interesting night."

Anita looked over the glass as she sipped her Old Fashion. She couldn't believe her luck. Anita's fate would be a dastardly night.

***

The bloody soapy water coursed down between perfect small breasts seaming to connect the freckles on the thing's chest. The shower water ran its course, slopping over the fiend's tight abdomen. The soap and water clung to the creature's slim thighs running haphazardly down into the tub's drain. The miscreation rinsed the soapy water from her long red hair before bending down and turning off the spigot. Stepping out of the shower, an abomination completely unfettered of humanity hugged the towel against her breasts, and ran a dainty hand over the fogged over mirror. She turned her head left and right looking for any blood or human skin debris clinging to the cute oval face. Green eyes stared back. The mirror cast a picture of a pert nose and full lips; a thing of beauty on the outside, rotten to the core underneath the human trappings. The only flaw on the pixie perfect countenance was a small crease in the middle of its forehead. The monstrous female called itself Myra.

Choosing a purple toothbrush, Myra brushed her human like teeth. Scrounging around in the vanity's cabinets, Myra found a hairdryer. She hummed loudly as she blow-dried her red hair. First, she flipped her luxurious hair forward, brushing and blow-drying the back of her hair. She flipped her head upright, and followed the brush strokes with the dryer until her hair was a silky sheen. Putting the hair dryer down in the sink, she began pulling open drawers searching for makeup. Applying eyeliner and a small bit of mascara, she moved on, taking special care to outline her voluptuous lips with pale pink lipstick. Dropping the towel to the bathroom floor, she moved into the bedroom completely naked. She passed by the bed and stepped into a pool of blood. Getting agitated, she rubbed the blood off her foot into the clean carpet in front of the master bedroom's walk-in closet.

Picking cotton dresses from hangers, she pressed them to her form looking for the right fit. Slowly, a pile of dresses accumulated on the floor. Finally, she picked a sun dress with large printed yellow flowers. She shrugged the dress on over her head. Searching the top shelf, she found a pair of clogs that were only half a size too big for her feet. The primordial creature moved back into the bedroom and took only a cursory glance at the grisly scene of her ghoulish handiwork.

Human blood saturated the bed, a nude body with the rib cage torn open to the side and poking up into the air like a grotesque fin. A woman lay broken in the middle of the bed pillows, her pericardial cavity completely emptied. The legs splayed out, and bruised arms opened wide. The woman's face wore a mask of horror. Her dead eyes bulging had created tears swimming through the pools of blood on her cheeks.

Myra walked down the hallway into the kitchen. Hanging by a magnet on the refrigerator door, a polaroid picture of the girl on the bed had "Anita's Birthday Bash" scrawled on the bottom. Anita's face in the picture smiled smugly at the camara. Opening the refrigerator, Myra pawed through bottles of soda, beer, and water bottles. She settled on a carbonated water. Tipping the sixteen-ounce bottle up, she finished it in two gulps. Her neck bulged unnaturally as she gulped. Dropping it carelessly to the floor, she then left the refrigerator door open. Spotting the woman's purse on the kitchen table, she riffled through it. A couple hundred dollars in bills tucked away in the back of the purse was her reward. She crumpled up the bills and slipped them into the back of her shoe. The animalistic thing peered around for more valuables as it walked through the house and out the front door into the bright sunshine of midday.

Chapter Three

Ida touched the glass door idly. She ignored the black and red sign proclaiming the shop to be closed. She did flinch when the cow bell rang out. She scanned the room, and saw the back door slightly ajar. Walking briskly through the store, she pushed the back door open, stopping for a moment as the sun beat down into her eyes. Of course, Sandra was sunbathing half nude in the back yard.

Dozing in the bright sunshine and wearing only the bottom half of a sky-blue two-piece bathing suit, Sandra's skin glowed pink underneath the heavy sun tanning oil. Sweat and oil made her breasts shiny. The fine blonde hairs on her stomach glistened in the sun's rays. Her legs splayed out to touch the bars on either side of the cheap lounge chair and she had her feet cocked to either side. She looked perfectly at home in her garden.

The garden had been a problem for the city council members when first discovered by a postal worker. They complained about drainage problems and the sewer line being too exposed to the weather. Sandra had calmly told them she had ripped out all the concrete with pick axes and small tools to bare earth. She backfilled the area with top soil and recovered the sewage line, making an oasis in the middle of town. She covered the soil with sod and planted flowers on one side and a small fruit tree on the other side. She gave them examples of how the rain water runoff would not interfere with the drive way in the back alley. The county administrators finely acquiesced after they realized it would cost the city money to pour a concrete pad back into place.

"Aren't you worried about kids skulking down the alley to take a peek?" asked Ida from the doorway.

Sandra cocked her head up and replied, "Hasn't happened yet. By the way, have you heard from Anita lately? Her romance novel came in today and she's not answering my texts."

Ida playfully squatted down on the grass next to Sandra, and replied, "No, but you know how busy she is and all that. By the way, I met some more interesting people in your charming little town. Makes me wonder why I didn't look for work in the northeast."

"Plum, if you are having problems with the yokels, I have a solution," said Sandra, sitting up.

"Shots!" exclaimed Sandra and Ida at the same time.

They both giggled for a moment. Sandra swung her legs over the side of the lounge chair, and said, "Just give me a couple of minutes to freshen up and take a shower. Larry's Bar isn't going anywhere."

"Thank god it's Friday," said Ida.

"Or the goddess," replied Sandra as she stepped through the doorway on her way upstairs to shower and change clothes.

Larry's Bar and Grill looked like a seedy joint. A gravel parking lot, tin roof, and a building with low walls tucked back from the road. To look at it, you would imagine the motorcycles parked outside the entrance as a warning sign. In reality, Larry kept the bar friendly and relaxed. Until eight or nine, families would come in and enjoy excellent seafood and maybe batter beer fries. After nine the kitchen closed, and the regulars poured in on a Friday night. The record player juke box would start playing, and the bartenders understood what a Cosmo was even if the locals ordering it didn't. A mixture of hard drinkers and college kids frequented the bar. Upstairs, you could hear pool balls colliding with each other. Downstairs, cafeteria tables were set up to hold the patrons. A couple small tables scattered throughout made the place homey. The lack of ventilation and windows made it a dive bar.

A battered Indian motorcycle pulled up to the entrance of the bar. Knocking the kick stand into place with a shod biker boot, Motorcycle Mamma pivoted off the old bike. Her black hair in two long pony tails reaching down her back was braided to keep the wind from tormenting her hair while riding at top speed. Her t-shirt printed with a rebel flag and a silhouette of an M-16 had a vernacular at the bottom stating "Cold Dead Hands". She wore faded blue jeans with an NRA patch on the back pocket. On one hip clung a small purse attached to her belt. On the other hip, a nine-inch double bladed knife in a scabbard that looked well worn. Not a small woman, she looked like what they say in the country as corn fed.

Motorcycle Mamma walked up to the entrance of the bar after depositing her bike, and held the door open for two women, saying "Sandra. Ida."

Both chimed, "Susan!" as they walked into the dimly lit bar. Sandra called out, while passing the bar, "Two shots of tequila, and two margaritas."

Sandra and Ida meandered through the tables of the bar nodding and smiling at the people they knew by name. In the corner, a fluorescent beer sign hung on the wall above a small table with two chairs occupied by one young man. Sandra stood at the edge of the table with her hands on her hips and said, "Excuse me sir, but you are sitting at our table."

The young man with shaggy brown hair replied with a smile, "Now, is that the way you treat our country's veterans?"

"I'll be, Jeffrey Morgan!" laughed Sandra. "You better stand up and give me a hug."

"Call me Jeff," he said, standing up and hugging Sandra. Jeff stood six feet tall. He seemed lanky with long arms and legs. He had an even smile and bright green eyes.

Sandra, testing the sound of it, said slowly, "Jeff?" She smiled and said quickly, "Meet Ida."

"How do you do?" answered Jeff. "You mind sharing the table?"

"Of course not, hunt down another chair," answered Sandra as the waitress brought the girl's drinks to the table.

While hunting for another chair, Jeff said, "Put that on my tab, Marti."

As Ida and Sandra sat down, Sandra said, "Watch out Ida, Jeff is a hoodlum of the ninth degree. His daddy is the county sheriff."

"Well, war has a way of tempering a man," replied Jeff with sad eyes. Smiling slowly, he said, "Fill me in on all the small-town gossip."

Jeff only listened half-heartedly to Sandra's chatter. The things she said seemed small. Being a veteran had taken a toll on Jeff. His small-town values were still secure, but fighting in Lebanon had irrevocably changed him. He had been wounded two times. An indiscriminate shot fired over the barricade had scarred his left bicep. Sixteen stitches later, his arm bore a jagged scar. A hand grenade had shattered his tibia and lacerated his lower extremities. A new surgery saved the bone. The G.I.'s called it a bone sock. Basically, a cylindrical shaped mesh was attached at the jagged portions of the missing bone.

Osteocytes clung to the mesh forming new bone where none existed. He was in traction for four weeks as his leg slowly healed. The biggest wound was in his heart. He had lost friends and seen monstrous atrocities in the war. All he wanted now was to slowly mend the holes he felt in his mind. He hoped coming home would do the trick.

Ida could not stop smiling all night long. Jeff entertained the two women with his youthful exploits. Like the time Jeff and some friends jumped a farmer's fence to gather psychedelic mushrooms. Unbeknownst to them, the farmer had left a young bull in that part of the field. The bull gave the band of kids a merry chase before they escaped over the fence. Sandra would recall some particular episode of Jeff's misspent youth, and he would have to explain his actions. Marti was kept busy all night long bringing drinks to the table. The world seemed to condense around just the three of them that night.

With a knowing smile, Sandra excused herself before the bar closed. Ida and Jeff ordered more drinks after Sandra left. Jeff, feeling bold, whispered in Ida's ear his intentions. Ida kissed him on the cheek and grabbed his hand, leading him out of the bar. Both of them chattered nervously as Ida drove her car to her small apartment just outside of the town limits. Ida ran up to the door fumbling with the keys, and Jeff stood nervously by her side with his blood coursing through his veins.

Ida opened the door, and the pair kissed while undressing. Shirtless, the pair stumbled into the back bedroom. In his haste, Jeff pulled down his pants before taking off his shoes. Ida laughed and pushed him onto the bed. She grabbed both shoes at once and pulled them free. Grabbing the cuffs of Jeff's pants, she whipped off his jeans. She stood there for just a moment, letting her eyes take in the details of his naked body. She dropped his jeans, and shrugged out of hers. She leapt on top of him laughing.

Afterwards, the pair lay sprawled upon the bed breathing heavily and feeling spent. Their blood sang in their ears. Both glistened in sweat, the air conditioning could not keep the summer heat from accumulating on their bodies. As they lay on their back breathing hard from the exertion, they held hands between their naked forms.

Jeff was the first to break the moment, and said, "I thought that would be different."

Ida yanked her hand from his, and retorted, "What, because I am brown?"

Jeff leaned on his elbow, and replied, "I didn't mean anything by it. That's just how guys think. Guys just think it's exotic. It would mean no different if you were Japanese."

"You're comparing me to some Japanese porn?" asked Ida. Staring at him for a moment, Ida said, "What you just said sounds childish." Ida felt indignant.

Feeling sheepish, Jeff replied, "Ida…"

"Don't Ida me." She pulled the covers over her naked form. "Just get out."

"Ida please," said Jeff holding his clothes after getting out of bed. "I didn't mean anything by it."

"Just leave," said Ida, facing away from him. "Just go."

Before leaving, Jeff said in a quiet voice, "I'm sorry."

When Ida heard the apartment door slap into place, she started crying. She cursed out loud her feelings of being alone. She hugged the pillow in her arms, falling into a fitful sleep and wishing that just for once Jeff had been different from so many other men in her life.

The same night, Myra sat in a restaurant chair with her back slightly arched pushing her small breasts against the fabric of a light blue camisole. Myra's red hair gathered in a ponytail made the freckles on her face seem perky as she smiled at the man sitting across from her. She sported white shorts riding on her hips. Blue sandals clad her elfin feet with hot red painted toe nails peering out of the leather open toe sandals. Every man in the restaurant peered over wine glasses, or glanced for seconds over upraised napkins to catch a glimpse of Myra.

The man, nervously holding a fork with chubby fingers, felt incredibly uncomfortable in the restaurant. His name was Dan Sloan. He wore a red and green Bahama shirt with blue jeans. He thought the shirt would be festive for the occasion. The colors just enhanced his pale lifeless skin, especially his jowls. Dan was a recluse. He rarely stepped outside his apartment and away from his fax machine. He worked from home as a medical transcriptionist. In his spare time, he played role playing games with a couple of teenagers in his neighborhood. He imagined the dice clacking on the table top as he rolled for initiative. He wished he could roll the dice to perform more admirably at the moment with the woman sitting across from him. He imagined his charisma in the game would surface in the conversation with the beautiful woman, but his ineptitude with real women hindered him. His only outside contact with the opposite sex was belonging to a coven who accepted his peculiar habits. His personal advertisement in the local paper for company had gone unanswered for two years. He could not fathom why a beautiful girl like Myra had contacted him. His loneliness persuaded him to accept an offer of dinner from a complete stranger.

Dan, seeking a way to start a conversation, said, "I didn't think women liked Steak Tartare." He quickly replied, "I mean, people in general."

Myra smiled and replied, "I like things that are messy."

Trying to keep the conversation flowing, Dan asked, "Is there something wrong with the baked potato? If it's cold, we can send it back to the kitchen."

Smiling again, Myra replied, "No, the potato is fine. I'm just on an all-protein diet."

Looking for an excuse to compliment her, Dan said, "I don't think you have to worry about that. I mean, diet."

Myra held up her hand in front of her mouth, and giggled, before she said, "How sweet."

"Ahh, well then," said Dan nervously fidgeting in his chair. "Thank you." He stared at his plate for a moment. "So, what do you do for a living?" Inside his mind, he groaned for asking such a boring question.

Holding the Steak Tartare in front of her mouth, she replied, "I'm a model." She quickly stuck the fork in her mouth before saying anything more on the subject.

"Wow, I mean, I guess you would be," exclaimed Dan. "I mean, you're so pretty." He groaned inwardly again, because he stated the obvious. Dan figured the date was not going well. He wondered if he should continue with the humiliation and order dessert. He decided to ask her about dessert. If she wanted to escape the situation, passing on dessert would be a way of ending the date. "How do you feel about dessert?" asked Dan attentively. He held his breath waiting for an answer.

Myra popped the last morsel in her mouth; slowly chewing on the piece of raw meat as she smiled at Dan before swallowing. Slightly parting her lips, she inhaled through her mouth; she could taste on her tongue the stench of magic emanating from Dan. Leaning forward, and placing her hand on Dan's thigh under the table, she answered, "Let's have dessert at your place."

Clothes spread out on the living room floor of Dan's apartment; a shirt on the couch, a sock on the table, and panties on a chair. The apartment remembered the echo of laughter as Myra lead Dan by the hand into the bedroom. Everything in the home lay perfectly still as if all the trappings of a lonely man had been abandoned. The home was eerily quiet. A compressor for the refrigerator kicked on sounding loud and out of place.

Myra straddled the corpse slowly licking the blood off her hand with a long sinuous tongue. Her tongue split down the middle, each moving on its own accord like tentacles. The fleshy pair independently wiggled while rooting out the blood between her fingers. She smiled and looked down upon the horrified face of Dan. She had ripped his throat out with her human like teeth right before he culminated in ecstasy; robbing him of even that simple pleasure before he died. A piece of his liver lay on his chest. Myra had found she was uncomfortably full from the earlier dinner, so had not finished her meal of the entrails of Dan. She felt disheartened that she could not fully empty the abdominal cavity. She decided not to be gluttonous. She thought, besides, there were more meals in the immediate future.

Chapter Four

Sandra bent over a cardboard cutout of a haunted house; trying in vain to get the cheap flimsy tabs to fit in small recessed holes. The latest pulp fiction novel lay in a small stack next to the cutout. This was supposed to be the easy part, building a recessed shelf in the middle of the stand. The cowbell clanged as someone walked into the store. Holding on precariously to the stiff cardboard, she looked over her shoulder at her customer.

"Stop staring at my ass, and help me with this thing," she said to Jeff. Jeff rushed over and grabbed the other end of the shelf. Between the both of them, the shelf popped into place. Sandra stood up and stretched the cramped muscles in her back. "Be a darling, and load the shelf with those books," said Sandra as she moved to the counter. She grabbed a glass of iced tea, and took a long pull from it. She turned around and took a gander at Jeff's tight butt.

Jeff stood up, after filling the shelf. Turning around, he half-heartedly smiled at Sandra, and said, "So, how bad did I screw up with Ida?"

Sandra pursed her lips, and said, "Bad, but maybe recoverable. You made a good impression at first." Sandra took another sip of the iced tea, and then said, "Flowers, chocolate, and a love poem should do the trick."

Jeff smiled and asked, "Chocolate, flowers, and my favorite love song?"

Sandra waved her hand, and said, "Boys. Whatever happened to the composition of love?"

"Blame it on Miss Gordan, my third-grade English teacher," answered Jeff. "She read my love poem to her out loud in class."

"Ouch," replied Sandra. "That was cruel and unusual punishment. Seriously, if you are really interested, a token would be thoughtful for Ida. A heartfelt apology would not hurt either." Changing the subject, Sandra asked, "So, you going to buy a book for being a jackass since I introduced you to Ida?"

"You got a book on how to write poetry?" asked Jeff.

"Smart ass, but now you've been caught." Sandra reached up on a shelf next to the cash register and brought down a book. Holding it up for Jeff to see, the book promised the reader to teach them simple poetry. She put the book in a plastic bag with Boundless Books embellished on it in pink. "Five dollars, please," she said holding out the bag.

Jeff knew he could say no, but he also knew being a shop owner was not easy. He thought of it as a peace offering. He knew that even though Sandra did not show it, she was disappointed in him for his behavior with Ida. Jeff dug out a five-dollar bill from his wallet, and exchanged goods with Sandra.

Feeling a little guilty, Jeff changed the subject, and said, "You want to hear something weird?"

Sandra hopped onto the counter and crossed her legs at the ankles, and said, "I always want to hear something weird."

Smiling with his eyebrows raised, Jeff said, "The boys in the lab in Columbia are all in a tizzy. My father sent them a bit of evidence in a murder case."

"Murder! Who was murdered?" asked Sandra.

Jeff waved his hand and said, "Just some guy. But listen, the evidence was a fingernail. They knew it was a fingernail because it had a clear coat polish on it. Anyway, the lab boys got all excited because they could not figure out what it was made of. You know, the fingernail. Seems as if an entomologist figured it out, he said it was made of an organic metal. He focused a beam of electrons onto the fingernail to read the x-ray spectrum. It turned out, the fingernail was enriched with zinc making it sharp and hard. The only other thing with organic metal is a fig wasp."

"Wow, that is incredible! I mean, who could have metal fingernails?" Sandra kicked her feet, and asked, "The murder didn't happen in our town, did it?"

"No, it was some guy named Dan Sloan."

Sandra stopped her feet, "Dan Sloan? I know that guy." What she almost blurted was he belonged to her coven. "Listen, I need to talk to your dad. Dan didn't have any living relatives."

"Yeah, I know. He's slated for the county furnace to be cremated."

"Cremated, no, he has a family plot in Georgia. Call your dad, I'm going to close up shop." Sandra punched a key on the register to open it. She put the five-dollar bill in a slot, and grabbed the store keys. "We'll figure it out when we get to your dad's office. You drive, let's go."

Chapter Five

The grave had been dug earlier that day with a modern machine. Filled in without a eulogy, the machine operator figured Dan Sloan had no friends or family. The machine operator finished the job. As he walked from the back of the warehouse, he sipped a beer trying not to think of the vacancy of his own friends and family.

A crescent moon crested over the line of trees surrounding the cemetery. Monolithic stones in neat rows adorned a hill. Winding up the hill, eleven people in single file held in hand lit white candles, the light straining to keep the dark at bay. Following each other, they amassed at the fresh grave site. In a loose circle, the eleven people stood motionless. A fresh wind rustled the candle light. Each person wore a black cape with unique ornaments clasping the top of the cape at the neck.

The coven stood in silence. No one spoke a word. The silent vigil meant the dead had a chance to speak to the individuals through memories. No human trappings, no agenda, and no eulogy were offered. The coven understood that death had taken one of their own members. They would console each other at a different moment. At the grave side, they understood Dan Sloan deserved the full attention of how he had affected every member of the coven without posturing for their own limited mortality.

Natalie Alkaev snuffed her candle out with her fingers. The last fond memory of Dan was him giving her a Russian book of poetry. She realized Dan had meant for her to embrace her Russian heritage. Being tall, athletic, and her skin milky white, her beauty was nearly flawless. The rest of her own and society's expectations were harder to meet. Her Russian parents tried to make her into an American woman. She went to a good private school. Given every chance to excel, she missed something in her life. Dan tried to show her that she was more than the sum of her accomplishments. Natalie could not attain anything of value because she always searched for her perfect match. Unconsciously, she pursued perfection in all aspects of her life. Never allowing mistakes by the men she dated meant she was always alone. Natalie walked to her car vowing to look beyond her vanity.

Kelly Brook brought the candle to her lips, and blew out the flame. As the small trail of black smoke curled around the bridge of her nose, she smiled thinking about Dan telling her to be more confident in her intelligence. Kelly was all curves in all the right places. Men eyed her like candy. She embraced her sexuality. She had manipulated men with sex. She reveled in sex; she never once apologized for being a sexual creature. Dan just wanted her to realize there was also something more than sex that needed nurturing. She turned and walked away from the group.

Mary Quarles painted a small smile on her face. She stood silently gazing down at the candle. Slightly overweight with brown hair dyed yellow, her self-esteem was a good match to her appearance. She always tried to fit in with any situation but she never seemed to be comfortable. Dan had repeatedly told her to be herself, and not what people expected of her. He was a dear friend to her. She would miss him greatly. She vowed to take his advice, and try living for herself. She walked away from the group holding the lit candle; trying to gain confidence in her life. Dan would want it that way for her.

Henry Stapper forcefully blew the candle out and walked briskly away from the grave site. Tears streaming down his face, he remembered coming to grips with being a portly homosexual. The first person he confided in was Dan. After Henry's mother died, Henry felt the need to finally tell someone. Scared of being ridiculed, Henry had confided to the one person who already knew his sexuality. More than once, Dan had willingly let Henry sate his sexual desire during the trials of a ritual. Henry knew Dan was not a homosexual, but Dan had not once stopped Henry from expressing himself. Henry decided that night to call his sister and declare his homosexuality. Dan would want Henry to be honest with himself and the world.

Paula Tulle moved away from the group and sat on a park bench watching the emotions of her friends. The oldest person in the coven, Dan had sought her out for advice more than once. Dan had been a kind man. Paula had loved him deeply, but never confessed her desire. She had thought the age difference had set them apart. She was sixty-two. Now she realized she had missed something tangible in life by not saying I love you. Her heart broken, she cried with small sobs. She felt resentment for life itself. She had thought her own death would have come long before Dan's. She had not wanted to love him and then leave him alone in the world. She could feel the comic tragedy of life. She consoled herself in knowing Dan loved her as a dear friend and confidant.

Sally Ann O'Conner had never been fond of Dan. She had found him boring like so many men before him. Blonde, petite, and cute, men had paid special attention to her. She had found each man lacking something. Coming to an epiphany, she realized turning thirty years old this year meant she was alone. Her intolerance of men had left her alone. Dan had tried on more than one occasion to make her realize loving someone would improve her life. It had taken his death for her to realize the importance of the life lesson he had tried to impart to her. She had never once felt lonely in life. The fawning men had always filled the gap of loneliness, but for once she realized she wanted an equal partner to share the precious few moments in her life. She could never tolerate a mooning kind of love, but she just now realized she had been missing something important about life, a sharing of sorts.

Cherie Hortman had a small sad frown on her face. The frown looked out of place. Always cheerful; she invested her whole life to helping people. Being a yoga instructor, her tight ebony body had driven more than one man to distraction. She was not some ditz who saw life through a colorful glass window. She just preferred to live life openly and honestly. Her emotions were always at the surface. She just felt whole while helping others realize their potential. She would miss Dan, but he had really never made an impact to her life. The problem was no one had made an impact on her life. She was too busy trying to help others; she never had the time to reflect about her own life. Dan had not changed anything in that respect. She continued to distance herself from introspection. She broke from the group, and headed to her car.

Muriel Stamos looked like a fifties pin up girl, black hair surrounding an angelic face. Ironically, she herself was in her mid-fifties. An artist, she was a photographer. She was well liked in the artist community, so she freelanced for several regional newspapers. Her critically acclaimed work dealt with nature. The nature photographs were very popular. Out of the coven, she was the richest individual in the group. Everyone knew she was loaded, including Dan Sloan. He had advised her on technology-based stock in the market. His advice had proven worthwhile. She thought of Dan as being an old soul. More than once his intuitive leaps about relationships had saved her from embarrassment and frustration with men. She trusted everyone, but most of all she trusted Dan. He had been a dear friend and confidant. She thought this as she snapped a picture of his head stone with a small camera. The picture would not see the light of day, as other pictures she had stashed away that chronicled her life. She walked to her car, her eyes always searching for the next picture. She knew Dan would always want that from her.

    Linda Magetti waited for one more moment before leaving the group at the grave site. Quick with her temper, she had more than once verbally berated Dan for being a buffoon. She thought of him as having no spine. He did not stand up for himself. He complained about life without actually living it. She found him intolerable as a person, a man of little vision. As she jerked the car door handle, she realized her anger. She was angry at Dan. She stopped and stared at the front seat of her car searching her conscious. She shook her head, and got in the driver's seat never figuring out at that moment what had made her so angry about Dan. Dan would haunt her memories for the rest of her life. He was the most forgiving person Linda had ever known, while she could never forgive herself for her own temperament. Her temper was like fire. It consumed everything in her life leaving only ash behind.

    Ida Makmur had waited until everyone had left. Having known Dan, the least amount of time, her impression of him lacked any real sympathy other than the loss of one of the witches coven. She had waited to talk to Sandra. She tried to gauge Sandra's reaction if she broke the silence. Ida decided to wait in the parking lot out of respect for Dan and Sandra. She had traded with Jeff for information about the two murders. Ida walked to her car folding the cape into a small square with the silver Mocking Bird clasp centered in the middle. She hoped the information would shed some light on the two murders.

    Sandra walked to the foot of the grave and stared at the head stone. As High Priestess of the coven, she was responsible for the lives of its members. She had lost two on her watch. She vowed not to lose any more. The responsibility weighed heavy on her heart. Sandra had been forewarned. When the last High Priestess had passed the mantle on to Sandra, she had been warned that death could visit any member of the coven. Dark forces have harassed witches for generations. To impart the serious matter of protecting the coven, the old High Priestess had told Sandra a gruesome story about the death of a coven member during the old High Priestess's watch. The story flittered through Sandra's mind. Sandra recalled the story to build mental strength for the upcoming fight with the monstrous enemy that had taken the lives of two from the matriarchal family.

The old High Priestess told Sandra a horrible tale about a Blood Witch. Blood Witches meddled with dark forces. Blood Witches were notorious for manifesting demons. All witches knew another plane of existence paralleled our universe. Most of the power garnered by witches came from this other plane of existence. Scientists called the ethereal plane a multiverse. Blood Witches opened gateways to allow monstrous animals to come to this earthly plane. The monstrous animals were known as demons. The Blood Witches subjugated the demons to their will, but sometimes the Blood Witches would be overwhelmed by powerful creatures not meant for this plane. Almost always in that instance the demon would kill the Blood Witch, and then walk the earth.

A Blood Witch named Vivian had been slighted by one of the men in the old High Priestess's coven years ago. Vivian's advances had been spurned by the young man. In retaliation, she summoned a demon to kill him. Sandra had asked the High Priestess why Vivian had gone to such an extreme. The High Priestess told her Vivian's gruesome story of growing up as an explanation for her cruel insanity.

The Blood Witches' powers are derived from the sacrifice of flesh, muscle, and bone. They alone work with the manna of dead or living carcasses of animals. Some of the most powerful spells had been derived from human sacrifice. In a pinch, Blood Witches have used their own blood. One of the ways to identify a Blood Witch was the keloid scars on their forearms. They cut themselves sporadically to use their hideous magic when a sacrifice was unavailable. Vivian's mother, Virginia, had been a Blood Witch of considerable power. Virginia used a small boy.

Virginia kidnapped a child from a school playground. Tony had been six years old at the time. Tony had made the national news due to the circumstances of the kidnapping. An unseasonable fog had covered the playground for a couple of minutes. The child caregivers said Tony had disappeared in the mist.

Virginia locked Tony in the basement. Vivian's chores when she became a pubescent teen were to feed, clean, and monitor the boy's health. Virginia used Tony as a living sacrifice. Virginia started with Tony's toes. She sliced off each toe for a dark spell. Working up each leg, Virginia for a decade amputated Tony's legs up to his knees for her diabolical spells. Unknown to Virginia, the physical torment and anguish endured by the boy married with the mental abuse endured by Vivian created a bond between the children. Vivian murdered her mother to free her little brother Tony.

To defeat her mother, Vivian used the flesh from Tony's right leg. While stripping the skin from his leg, Vivian made a vow to Tony this would be the last time anyone would cut meat from his legs. Using the very spells Virginia had taught her daughter, Vivian summoned a demon to kill her mother. She used the same deadly demon to also murder the young man in the old High Priestess's coven years later. Vivian cut off the last finger from Tony's right hand to accomplish that murderous task.

Sandra figured the world was a cruel place.

Sandra walked back to the parking lot lost in thought. Before getting into her car, Ida stepped out of the peripheral corner of her eye. Ida just stood there waiting to see if Sandra was going to acknowledge her. Sandra shut the car door, and walked behind the old seventies beetle. Leaning against the warm exterior portion of the covered motor, Sandra gestured for Ida to join her.

"Hell of a night," said Ida. "Too bad we could not congregate at Anita's grave site."

"Harder than you would think," answered Sandra. "Anita's grandparents took her back to Canada to be cremated." Sandra stopped for a moment, and then asked, "What did you find out from Jeff?"

Ida leaned against the rear well tire panel, and said, "He didn't want to tell me anything at first when I called him. It was hard to track him down. Apparently, he doesn't have a place to call his own. But we made a deal, information from his father's notes about the case for a date at the Midnight Bowling Lanes in Columbia."

"Are you giving him another chance?" asked Sandra.

"Maybe," answered Ida. "I mean, I don't know."

Sandra patted Ida on the shoulder, and said, "If anything here tonight meant anything. Life is short."

"Yeah, well, anyway," said Ida shrugging her shoulders. "Jeff did tell me after I agreed to go on a date with him that the only physical evidence was a long red strand of hair at both crime scenes. One hair on Dan's side of the bed, and some loose hairs in Anita's hairbrush. They also found the weird fingernail as well. The cops are stumped."

"Well, that is a beginning and the cops here are Mayberry," Sandra paused for a moment, and then asked, "When is the date?"

"Tomorrow night," answered Ida. "Woohoo, beer and crappy fries for dinner." Both of them giggled, and then sighed at the same time.

Chapter Six

Ida wanted the date night at the bowling lanes to be a bust, but Jeff was just too charismatic. Ida enjoyed the silly jokes, and the way Jeff looked at her. She would catch him out of the corner of her eye just staring at her with a small smile on his face. It felt good to be around someone so popular. Several people during the night would come up to Jeff and chat briefly with him. He just seemed to know everybody, and he always introduced her to the people. He included her in every conversation. She had never felt so whole; maybe because she felt a little drunk from the cheap beer.

Ida carefully rolled the bowling ball down the lane. The last thing she wanted to do was slip and fall in front of Jeff. Bowling had become more difficult due to the cheap beer in the plastic cups. They were only on the fourth frame of the third game. Several pins fell over slowly as if also drunk. Ida clapped her hands, and turned in a small circle. Jeff stood at the ball release station waiting his turn with a big grin on his face.

Ida sashayed up to Jeff. Leaning against Jeff with her whole body touching his, she whispered into his ear, "I could use a cigarette."

"I thought you didn't smoke," said Jeff.

"Only when I am a little tipsy," replied Ida flicking her finger across his chin.

Jeff scanned the crowd for any employees of the bowling alley. He grabbed the two cups full of beer, and said, "They won't allow us to go out with beer in our hands, but we can take the emergency exit to the alley."

Following Jeff, Ida asked, "But won't the alarm trip if we use the door?"

Pushing against the emergency door exit, Jeff answered, "It hasn't worked for years."

Both of them stepped into the alley beside the bowling lanes. Ida stretched her face towards the full moon, closed her eyes, and smiled. Jeff jammed an aluminum can in the door frame. Handing Ida her beer, he juggled his while lighting a couple of cigarettes.

The full moon cast a sharp shadow of the building. They were only twenty feet from the entrance of the alley, so they leaned against the building to keep in the shadows and mask drinking the beer.

Pulling a drag from the cigarette, Ida asked, "How can something so bad for you feel so good?"

Jeff leaned against the wall next to her, and said, "You might ask the same question when it comes to all vices."

Ida punched his shoulder lightly, and said, "Look at you, being the philosopher."

Jeff laughed and said, "Let's just say I know what bad is."

Ida dropped the cigarette, and snuffed it out with the toe of her shoe. Putting her hands against the wall with Jeff's head cradled in the middle, she leaned in close, and asked, "Just how bad are you?"

Jeff flicked his cigarette down the alley before grabbing Ida's hair. He pulled her head close to his, and kissed her full on the mouth. He felt Ida jerked away from his grasp. Ida hit the wall opposite Jeff, falling down to the pavement. A woman with red hair hovered in his view. Grabbing Jeff by the shirt, the red-haired woman tossed Jeff out of the alley onto the sidewalk as if he weighed nothing.

Myra cocked her head sideways as she looked back at Ida. The crease in the middle of her forehead opened slightly. Myra said, "What could an ugly duckling like you do to hurt me? The spell won't be enough." Myra reached out to grab Ida.

Ida had been funneling the sunlight from the full moon with her raised, outstretched hand. Murmuring an incantation, Ida finished the spell just in time as Myra reached down to grab her. Ida placed her hand in front of Myra's face and released the moonlight.

Myra staggered back blind from the sudden burst of bright light. Myra blinked her eyes, but could only see white spots.

Jeff rushed into the alley. A knife one and a half inches long was considered to be a utility knife, not a weapon. Today, the blade was a weapon. Jeff raised Myra's arm, and jammed the knife into her kidney.

Myra screamed an unholy sound, and pulled her arm free from Jeff's grasp. Myra staggered down the alley away from the entrance.

Jeff helped Ida to her feet, and said, "Damn that bitch is strong." Jeff started towards the street, and said, "We've got to get out of here."

Ida and Jeff stumbled into the parking lot lit by street lamps. Not feeling safe, they ran for the entrance of the bowling alley.

Myra leaned against the alley wall holding on to the jagged wound in her lower back. She blinked her eyes continuously until she could see more than spots of light.

"Hey lady, this is my alley. Get the hell out of here," said a drunk man. The old man's back was against the wall with his legs splayed out in front of him. He sipped on a pint of liquor. Wiping his mouth with a grimy sleeve, he glared up at Myra.

Myra smiled and approached the man. The man opened his mouth to say something, and Myra reached into his mouth and grabbed his tongue. Pulling the tongue far out of his mouth as the man screamed hollowly; Myra grabbed his lower jaw and forced the man's mouth shut. The man's teeth severed the tongue. The vagrant spit a fountain of blood. Scared, the old man clasped his hands over his mouth to stop the bleeding. He asphyxiated on his own blood.

Myra pulled up her blue blouse to get to the wound. Wringing out the tongue like a dish towel, Myra worked the warm blood deep into the wound. She sighed. The hole in her back side sealed shut, leaving an angry puckered scar. Myra tossed the tongue. The tongue landed precariously on the dead man's head. As she walked down the alley, she cleaned her bloody hand with her tongue.

In the bowling alley, Jeff ran to a bank of pay phones. Inserting a dime, he started to call his father.

"Jeff, wait," said Ida. "You can't report this to the police."

Jeff looked at her astounded, and said, "Why not, it's the right thing to do."

Ida took the phone and placed the receiver into its cradle, saying, "Your drunk, and you just stabbed a woman."

"But," stammered Jeff, "that could have been the woman who killed your friends!"

"Yes," replied Ida. "And by the time the police get here, she will be long gone. I need the knife, Jeff."

"What?" asked Jeff. He looked down to see the bloody knife still in his hand. He glanced around quickly, and closed the knife's blade. He stuffed it into his pocket. "Why do you need the knife?"

"I can't explain here. Right now, I mean," answered Ida.

"When, then?" asked Jeff.

"Just trust me. I will tell you later," she said with her palm up.

Jeff reached into his pocket, and handed her the knife. He said, "One hell of a date."

Ida patted his cheek and said, "But a fortunate one. This knife will prove useful."

Ida could not tell Jeff in public that the knife could be used to locate the creature. The spell would be complicated. Ida figured Sandra could use the blood on the knife to find the creature. As physically strong as the red-haired woman was, Ida believed it to be a creature.

"Can you take me home now?" asked Ida.

The black Nissan Z pulled into the parking lot of Ida's apartment building. Jeff found an unoccupied space and parked. He turned the engine off, and they just sat in the car for a moment.

Ida seemed about to say something to Jeff, but Jeff leaned over and kissed her. The kiss became very heated. Jeff pawed at her breasts. Ida grabbed his groin. Jeff undid the clasp of the bra strap through Ida's shirt with one hand. Neither Ida nor Jeff unlocked the kiss. Ida unbuttoned her shirt. Jeff's hands pushed the bra above her breasts. Jeff buried his face in the mounds of flesh. Ida gripped the back of his head and moaned. Jeff worked his way back to Ida's lips. Out of the corner of Ida's field of vision, a car pulled into a parking space across from them. She started giggling, which interrupted the kiss, and said, "I think we are a peep show."

Ida buttoned her shirt leaving the bra askew. She said, "Call me."

Jeff replied, "Absolutely."

"Tomorrow," said Ida.

"Of course," replied Jeff.

Smiling, Ida leaned over and kissed Jeff on the cheek. She opened the car door, and got out. Closing the door, she looked through the glass window and waved. She turned, and headed for her apartment.

The next day, Ida pushed open the door to Sandra's shop. The cow bell rang, and Sandra looked up. Sandra was with a customer. Sandra smiled and beckoned Ida to stay in the shop. Ida perused the latest gossip magazines next to the door. Ida only had to wait a moment before the customer left the building. Smiling, Ida walked up to the counter.

"For someone who was attacked last night, you look pretty smug," said Sandra. "I just got off the phone with Jeff. Off and on again, huh? Well, anyway, do you have the knife?"

Ida pulled a zip lock plastic bag out of her pocket. Setting the knife down on the counter, Ida asked, "Can you find her; or it?"

Sandra picked up the bag, and peered at the knife. She said, "I don't work with blood, but I know someone who does. I talked to her on the phone late this morning. She wants us to come up and see her tonight."

With a pinched face, Ida asked, "Who is it?"

Sandra put the knife back on the counter, and said, "A Grey Witch. She's old. My grandmother introduced me to her as a child." Sandra pushed the knife away from her, and said, "Magenta knows how to work with blood."

"Where are we going?" asked Ida.

"Up into the foot hills of the Blue Ridge Mountains," answered Sandra. "She lives as far north as you can get in South Carolina. It's only a two-hour drive." Sandra stared down at the knife and said, "But it should be worth it."

Ida peered out of the passenger side window of the yellow VW bug. At present, the curvy highway cut through a National Forest on the back roads of nowhere. Ida had seen from her window trailers, bungalows from the fifties, and almost palatial compounds of large farm houses set back from the road; the gambit of wealth from the very poor to the seemingly rich. South Carolina hoarded them all. Ida twisted uncomfortably in her seat. The trees on the side of the road seemed to hide an unknown force of nature.

Ida could not fool herself any longer; she was scared. Not the scared you feel when you walk into a party hoping to see someone you know, Ida felt truly terrified of dying. The thing with red hair made Ida envision her own mortality. She believed if Jeff had not been there, she would have died in that alley. A dirty stinking alley would have been her place of demise. She had always imagined dying in some relevant way; helping war torn children in another country, falling off a pyramid in Egypt, drowning in the sea as she explored an underwater vessel, not some stinking alley in the back of a bowling alley.

Ida tried to reevaluate her life; It seemed important considering she had almost died. The truth was depressing. She lived in a small town in South Carolina. She had never been on an adventure. She had always played it safe. In college, she told her friends spring break in Florida was too expensive; the truth was she did not want to take chances. The chance of being hurt, being afraid, and being alone meant Ida had played it safe for too long. She had been comfortable just riding the wave of life. Ida felt the pressure to take a chance for once in her life. At that moment, she thought about Jeff. Jeff expanded Ida's horizons. She realized Jeff meant more to her than she had thought. Ida felt Jeff might be worth taking that chance.

Ida shrugged her shoulders feeling a low sense of anxiety. She wanted to be adventurous, but meeting a Grey Witch made the nape hairs on the back of her neck stand on end. Grey Witches meddled with dark forces. Always in the name of scholarship, the Grey Witches explored dark paths. Always solitary, they usually went insane trying to balance the evil aspects of their work and keeping a firm grip on morality.

Ida came out of her reverie. She found herself looking at the buildings of a downtown area of a small town. Turning to Sandra, Ida asked, "Are we there yet?" Ida realized the immature joke, and laughed unexpectedly.

Chuckling, Sandra said, "Almost, Magenta lives a couple of blocks past the downtown area."

Sandra pulled into a driveway of a quaint little bungalow house. A small front porch with overflowing flower pots on each step, rose bushes planted on the front lawn and clovers lining the walkway up to the front steps made the house seem to have Southern charm.

Ida had pictured a sinister shack in the middle of the woods, not some old ladies house a shout away from downtown.

Ida followed Sandra up the walkway. The sun was still high in the sky in the late part of the summer, but it would not be long before the days became shorter. Ida shuffled her feet as Sandra knocked on the door.

The door opened slowly, and Ida smelled fresh baked apple fritters.

An old woman stood in the doorway. Magenta wore a checkered blue summer dress with white buttons marching up the front to her neck. Magenta's white hair was pulled back and pinned in place to make a tight bun on the back of her head. The wrinkles on her face gave her character. Her bony liver spotted hands spoke volumes about her age. Magenta smiled and motioned to the girls to come in through the door.

Magenta walked across an oriental throw rug in the atrium, and asked lightly, "Would you girls like some sweet tea?" Not waiting for an answer, Magenta walked to the back of the house where the girls imagined the kitchen would be in such a small home.

Ida glanced around the living room. The furniture was plush. A couch and chair had a similar pattern of big, if faded, flowers. All the tables in the room were walnut wood. The tables were dark in contrast to the patterned throw rugs of bright cheery colors over hardwood floors. Light in the room was scarce. Heavy brown curtains blocked most of the sunlight struggling to light the living room. Book shelves were situated in odd places around the room. The walls were adorned with cheap framed posters of Georgia O'Keeffe paintings.

Magenta walked out of the kitchen holding a silver platter with three glasses of tea, and a mound of apple fritters on a large, white, porcelain plate. A black cat danced around Magenta's feet. Magenta put the tray in the middle of the coffee table and sat heavily down on the couch. Sandra sat next to her, and Ida sat in the overstuffed chair across from them.

Clapping her hands lightly, Magenta then said, "Now dig in. It is a special occasion when I can talk freely about witchcraft."

Ida and Sandra sipped on their teas and munched on the apple fritters, still warm from the cast iron frying pan.

Finally breaking the girl's silence, Sandra, trying not to sound nervous, said "Do you remember my grandmother?"

"Oh, yes. She was a finicky old witch." Magenta smiled, and sipped her tea.

Ida cleared her throat and said, "It's nice to meet you."

Magenta put the glass of tea onto the table. Her eyes seemed dead for a moment, and then a twinkle of light escaped. She said, "Sorry, my manners are not so good. I spend most of my time alone except for talking to Bezzy. Ain't that right Bezzy?" She reached down and ran her hand across the cat's back.

Sandra pulled the knife from her pocket still in the plastic bag, and said, "Do you think you can locate it?" She handed the knife to Magenta.

Magenta turned the knife over and over in her hands, and said, "Sorry dear, not enough blood, but all is not lost. There is enough blood to tell us what "it" is. I have whipped up something to help us with that task. Be a dear, and hand me the rack of vials up on the book shelf."

Ida got up and found a small rack of vials placed on a shelf. Each of the vials was labeled. Curious, Ida read the labels before handing them to Magenta. From left to right, the vial labels read Human, Night People, Demons, and Faye.

Magenta put the rack on the coffee table next to the silver platter. Magenta took the knife out of the plastic bag, and opened the bloody blade. She placed the knife on the raised lip of the silver platter, balancing it in place with the handle on the curve of the tray and the tip gripping the circular curve edge of the silver tray.

First, Magenta grabbed the vial labeled human.

Ida interrupted Magenta, and said, "I know that thing was not human."

"No, child, but many things start out as human," Magenta said as she dripped liquid onto the blade. The liquid turned black. Magenta harrumphed, and said, "It is half human."

Magenta reached for the vial labeled Night People. She dripped the clear liquid onto the blade. The clear liquid ran off the edge without turning into any other color. "Well, it is not a werewolf or something else from the Night People."

Magenta handled the vial labeled Demons. She poured a small amount onto the blade. The liquid was unaffected. "It is not a human possessed."

Magenta carefully poured the vial labeled Faye onto the only part of the blade still dry. The clear liquid turned purple. All three witches leaned in and looked at the purple liquid. Magenta asked, "Bezzy, where is that book on Faye blood?"

The cat answered, "On the third shelf in the big book case."

Shocked, Ida sat up straight. Her nerves grated like steel wool on a frying pan. The cat was possessed by a powerful demon. Only the most powerful demons could talk after being trapped in the body of an animal. The cat seemed to react to Ida's fear. It began to purr loudly.

"Could you be a dear, and hand me the red book on the third shelf of that book case?" asked Magenta, pointing.

Ida hopped up and grabbed the book. She handed it to Magenta. Ida stood behind the oversized chair to keep her distance from the cat.

Magenta flipped the pages. She stopped half-way in the book. She read the text in a couple of minutes. She then clapped the book shut with one hand, and said, "A Grendel."

Ida asked, "Like in Beowulf?"

Sandra asked, "But, isn't the Grendel in Beowulf some kind of green monster?"

"Yes, and yes. But a female Grendel looks human. The only unhuman characteristic is said to be a third eye for seeing magic," said Magenta.

"I think I saw that. When I was performing a spell, a crease in her forehead seemed to open slightly," said Ida.

"Where does a Grendel come from?" asked Sandra.

"A Grendel comes from the debauchery of a witch and a satyr. If the witch survives the almost insatiable satyr, she is granted a hundred years of living in a stasis of youth; but she always gives birth to a Grendel," answered Magenta.

"How do you kill it?" asked Sandra.

"That's just it. You have to kill it and its mother. Also, the only way to kill a female Grendel is to bathe a silver blade in a victim's blood and bless the knife under a new moon for the Goddess Hekate," said Magenta.

"But both victims are buried and gone," said Ida.

Smiling, Magenta said, "Don't worry, dear. There will be another."

Chapter Seven

The sun had set on the yellow VW beetle on the back roads of South Carolina. Ida sat in the passenger side engrossed in her own thoughts. She should have been thinking about the Grendel, but her thoughts simmered about Jeff. Ida decided she liked him. His boyish charm, his rugged looks, and his intelligence made him an ideal boyfriend. But sometimes his face would relax and he seemed to go someplace in his mind that harbored shadows. He just seemed to brood on a subject. Ida asked where his mind was during that time. He would just smile and say nowhere. Simple things seemed to elicit a brooding response by Jeff. Ida thought he had a secret; maybe one day he would give her a clue.

The car slowed down to ten miles an hour on a desolate back road to nowhere. Sandra turned on her bright lights to pierce the darkness. She was searching for a mailbox on the side of the road with an American flag painted on both sides. Sandra nervously glanced in her rear-view mirror, afraid another car would come speeding down the road and smash into the back of the beetle. They cruised for a couple of miles before spotting the mailbox.

Sandra pulled the car onto a washed-out driveway. The driveway consisted of sand and gravel. Bumpy and unpredictable, the driveway wound into the woods. The beetle would bottom out every so often. Being a small car, the beetle had a good chance of straddling the washed-out road. Navigating left and right almost simultaneously on the road, they bumped down the dirt lane. Sandra and Ida held on as the car bounced and rocked down the dirt driveway. Sandra went slowly down the drive for several minutes. Turning at almost a ninety-degree angle, the driveway finally smoothed out into a large clearing.

The car headlights seemed dim compared to the fluorescent bulb mounted to the top of a large barn. Behind the barn, a single-wide trailer with a deck sat in shadow. Sandra stopped the car and beeped the horn a couple of times. Three German Shepherds ran up to the car barking loudly. Sandra and Ida sat in the vehicle and waited.

Ida asked, "You sure it's o.k. for us to be here?"

Sandra laughed and then said, "I know people think Motorcycle Mama is weird, but it's fine. She just likes her own privacy. Besides, I can't think of anyone else who would have a silver knife. Here she comes."

Susan wore a plain white t-shirt and khaki shorts. She walked up to the car and patted her thighs. The dogs immediately turned and went to her. Susan patted all three dogs on the head and then shooed them into the woods. She smiled and waved at the two girls in the car.

Sandra and Ida stepped out of the car. After closing the door Sandra said, "Susan, I hope it's not too late?"

"Nonsense, I was just watching my show. What brings you out here?" asked Susan.

Sandra replied, "We came to ask a favor."

"Sandra dear, as many times as you drove me home from Larry's Bar, I can't deny you anything," said Susan.

Sandra walked up to Susan and gave her a hug. Sandra gave her a summary of why they were there. Sandra told her about the Grendel, and why they needed a silver knife.

"I know silver is expensive right now, but maybe I can pay you in installments," said Sandra.

Susan frowned a little before saying, "Listen, I know what you are, like a lot of people in town do. If you say the thing in town that killed Anita is a monster, I believe you. Besides, Anita was my friend too. All I ask is that you keep a secret."

Ida asked, "A secret?"

Susan replied, "You will see. Follow me."

Susan walked up to the barn followed by the girls. The barn was a solid structure built of wood and steel. The double doors were large enough for a medium car to go through. The doors were made of wood and banded steel. A smaller steel door was recessed into one of the larger doors. Beside the small but intimidating door, an electronic key pad rested. Susan covered the key pad with her hand as she entered a numerical code. The door sprang open slightly with the sound of many locks unlocking. Susan turned and smiled at the girls before entering. The girls entered not knowing what to expect.

An M4 Sherman tank sat in the middle of the barn. Built in World War II, the tank could fire a round reasonably accurately as it trudged along on steel tracks. The front of the tank seemed to be blunt and rounded. The body of the tank swept back in a rounded angle like a bird's wing. The turret sitting on top was a round stunted hat with Pinocchio's nose extending out.

"Goddess, does that thing work?" exclaimed Sandra.

"It's the reason I bought forty acres of land," answered Susan. "I take her out every Sunday."

On the back wall of the barn, racks of military grade rifles hung on the wall. Several smaller rectangular racks held several handguns. A box in the corner was labelled grenades. Susan walked over to a trunk and opened it. She fished around and pulled out a knife with a scabbard.

Holding up the knife for the girls to see, Susan unsheathed the knife. Made of pure silver, the knife was over a foot long. The pommel, clad in wood with silver cross bars, was round. The blade extended out about ten inches. The blade was a sliver of silver. The blade was not flat. Instead, the blade was triangular extending into a sharp point. Not meant to cut, the knife was a weapon used to stab. The cross bars stopped your hand from slipping as you stabbed someone in the back. The slender triangular blade was sturdier than a flat knife so it could puncture muscle and viscera to pierce organs.

"A Venetian assassin's blade from the fourteenth century, meant to work its way into vital organs. The slim triangular blade is considerably stronger than a flat blade and can easily pierce the body," said Susan. She handed the knife to Sandra.

"Is it real?" asked Sandra.

"Yes, and very valuable," answered Susan. "Make it worth it. Stick it in the heart of that creature. I can't think of a better use for it."

Chapter Eight

Paula Tulle, the oldest member in the coven, stared at the coffee maker on the counter. She wore a pink robe over red pajamas. Her feet were in bunny slippers her niece gave her on her sixty-second birthday. Her grey hair in a fuss, she waited for the coffee to brew.

The kitchen looked like a throwback to the fifties. Red Formica counter tops with a band of silver aluminum were placed against the back wall with a stove and refrigerator to break up the flat surface. The floor was tiled in linoleum squares with soft yellow flower petals in the center of each square. The kitchen table with round aluminum legs and a red Formica top with a band of silver aluminum around the edge sat in the corner. The table was surrounded by chairs with red backs and red seats made from vinyl. The only thing missing was a soda fountain.

Without turning, Paula asked, "Would you like a bit of coffee?"

Myra strode into the kitchen. "What, no screaming? No running for the hills?"

"At my age, life scares you more than death. I can't remember a time when I enjoyed a TV program other than a rerun. The news brings death to the living room. People just don't talk anymore."

Myra replied, "And that is what you want to do, talk?"

Paula moved to the table with a couple of mugs of coffee. "Seems like a small thing to ask."

Myra sat in the chair opposite Paula with her knees under the table. She reached for the coffee and sipped on it without cream or sugar. "So, what do you want to talk about?"

"I could ask you why you are killing us." Paula took one sip of coffee and then put her hands in her lap. "But I don't know if you would answer truthfully."

"I might, considering you are about to die." Myra took another sip of coffee.

"First, let's start with a name," said Paula.

"But within a name you could find a clue," answered Myra. She sipped before answering. "My name is Myra McDonnel."

"McDonnel, McDonnel, that does sound familiar," said Paula.

"It is my mother's maiden name," answered Myra. She stopped talking abruptly. Myra reached across and flipped the table away from them. It crashed against the other wall of the kitchen.

Paula sat in the chair working her fingers deftly. The finger spell was almost complete. The table had been hiding something. A small black void hovered above the floor. It was as if nothing could exist there. No floor, no earth, no light; a hole that was a void like atoms did not exist in this world.

Myra stared at the void. "You could have not created that with just a finger spell. The spell took time to prepare."

"Yes, but I can complete the spell with my fingers."

"And, if I stop you?"

"Both of us will probably die."

Myra reached across. She grabbed both thumbs. Wrenching her hands, Myra broke both of Paula's thumbs with a quick jerk.

A terrible gale force of wind rushed for the void toppling both of them onto the floor. The rent in our universe closed abruptly after expelling a hurricane of air. Myra slid across the floor. Paula was thrown against the counter tops. Paula's right leg snapped when it struck the edge. Paula fell to the floor with a compound fracture to the femur. The white bone stuck out of her thigh. Paula just lay on the floor. Her face twisted in pain.

Myra stood over Paula. "At first, I had planned on killing you quick. I mean, you just seemed nice." Myra grabbed the exposed bone. She wiggled the bone.

Paula screamed. Her face sweating, Paula felt immense pain. She reached for Myra's hand. Myra batted her hand away. Paula grabbed the side of her thighs. Myra twisted the femur. Paula's head banged repeatedly against the floor. Myra shoved the bone forward ripping muscle as it leveraged against the thigh. The bone came out of the leg like pulling the bone from a chicken wing. The ragged hole in Paula's thigh ran with blood. Paula beat her hand against the cabinets while screaming. Paula's heart stopped.

Myra leaned down. She sucked the marrow from the femur before dropping it. She leaned her hand against the counter top, and looked into Paula's face. Smiling gleefully, Myra enjoyed the death mask of Paula's countenance. Myra leveraged herself up onto the counter top. Myra reached into the cabinet and grabbed a coffee mug. She poured the last bit of coffee from the overturned container.

"I hate for it to go to waste," said Myra to the ghastly vestige on the floor.

***

Hearing screaming from Paula's house, a neighbor had called the police. The police arrived, and put up the yellow tape. A couple of reporters from out of town had arrived because they knew it was a spree killing in a small town. The deputies kept them at bay, promising to answer questions at a later date. Two deputies stood in the carport not wishing to see the grisly scene in the kitchen. One of the deputies was an old man, hair white as snow. The other deputy was a rookie. Young but efficient, the man had his sights on being county Sheriff one day. The elected Sheriff of the county arrived. Mike Morgan looked like a Hollywood star. Tall, athletic, with fine blonde hair, Mike's countenance of rugged good looks would make most politicians jealous. The Sheriff had managed to win years of elections. Mike, the Sheriff, stood at the back door for a moment, took a deep breath and entered into the kitchen.

The kitchen was in shambles. It reminded the Sheriff of a scene after a tornado, except the wind had only touched the kitchen. The kitchen looked like someone had opened all the cabinets and emptied them upside down on to the kitchen floor. The Sheriff could not help but step on broken debris strewn across the floor. Blood was on the counter, the walls, even the ceiling. A bloody chef's knife handle protruded straight out of Paula's chest as if into a macabre butcher's block. Papers and dish towels were stuck to the bloody body. The Sheriff guessed the body had been rolled around in the debris.

Paula's body looked deflated from the waist down. Obviously, the femurs from her body had been plied from her thighs using the knife. The femurs were broken in two pieces and carelessly dropped beside the body. The Sheriff gingerly lifted one of the pieces, and peered into the bloody maw. The femur reminded him of an animal's kill. The marrow sucked from the bone. The Sheriff dropped the bone, and absently wiped the blood from his hand onto his pants.

Mike looked around the room without actually seeing anything but blurry fog since his mind could not wrap itself around what had actually happened in the kitchen. He was lost for a moment in his own thoughts. Trying to decide the best course of action escaped him since he felt way out of his depth. He decided, no, he would not have his small-town turn into a freak show. He would catch the bastard without the FBI or anyone else's help. There had to be a clue in this mess that would point him in the right direction. A neighbor must have seen something, but did not realize it's significance. Follow the clues, he thought, that was how he would catch this monster.

The next day, Ida and Jeff stood outside of the Conservatory, an auspicious name for a building with theater style seats facing a stage. The Conservatory was actually the only remaining building of a high school built in the Fifties. Most schools at the time had an auditorium as a separate building for school plays, assemblies, and pep squad gatherings. A band would play on the stage, cheerleaders would cheer, and principles would give rousing speeches. Now auditoriums were delegated to the gym with pull out bleachers in most high schools. The classic education of the youth was lost in the early nineteen eighties.

The city of Clear View had demolished all of the old high school buildings when the new, modern facility was built, except for the Conservatory. Now the building was used for concerts, plays, or anything else you wanted if you could pay the rental fee. The building served hot dogs, burgers, and tacos, as well as watered down beer. The guests ignored the bland beer because they were participating in a perceived high society function. A place for the locals to parlay with the rich residents of Clear View, the locals felt sophisticated in their pursuit of the Arts.

Jeff had invited Ida to the concert. The Merry Olde Time, a band with a banjo player, guitar player, a couple of female singers as backup, and a narrator performed eighteenth century music. Lovely songs such as Camptown Races and Swanee River, both written by Stephen Foster, filled the auditorium with the sounds of the past.

During the intermission, the couple walked out to their car for a cigarette. Chatting idly about the concert, the couple finished their cigarettes. Ida leaned in close for a kiss. Leaning against the car door, Jeff put his arms around Ida as they shared a smooch. Working in concert, Ida's and Jeff's tongues danced in each other's mouths. Ida placed a hand on Jeff's firm stomach. Working her hand into Jeff's waist band, she grabbed his hard shaft.

Coyly, Ida said, "What are you going to do with this?"

Jeff reacted by saying," Umm."

"Well, if you don't know what to do with it, then what am I supposed to do with it," said Ida. Ida let go, and said, "I'll try not to be a tease." Patting Jeff's cheek lightly, she said, "Back to earth."

Jeff just nodded.

"Listen, I have a favor to ask," said Ida. "Are you listening?"

Jeff grunted, "Yeah." Letting out a long breath, he then asked, "What's the favor?"

"I need to get into the city morgue, after hours, to see Paula."

"She's your friend. Why not just go during regular hours?"

"Do you really want to know, or can you do me this favor?"

Jeff stared over Ida's head for a moment, then answered, "How about tomorrow."

"Excellent. Let's go back to the concert, or I can show you what to do with this at my place," she said, poking him in the crotch.

Jeff opened the passenger door of the car and said, "Screw the concert."

As Ida sat down in the passenger seat, two cruel eyes watched from across the parking lot. Myra clenched her fist into a ball. Turning in her car seat in a rusted out blue Buick, she asked, "Momma, can I do it here?"

Turning the keys to the vehicle on, a young woman with old eyes said, "No. There are too many people."

The young-looking woman put the vehicle in gear and stretched her arm out to handle the wheel of the car as she backed up. Yellow street light made the keloid scars on her arm look sickly. She turned the wheel, draping her scars in shadow as she backed out of a parking space.

She glared at Jeff's car, then she turned down a side street; the Buick blending into the dark night as it disappeared.

Beside the Conservatory, in the shadow of the building, Sandra watched the blue Buick pull away. Sandra had been tailing Ida all night expecting something to happen. Nothing had, but now Sandra had more information. Apparently, there were two monsters in the night.

Chapter Nine

            The Sheriff's Office resided on Main Street at the end of the street. One of the original buildings constructed for downtown, the Sheriff's Office was the last building on the right headed north. The first story building faced the street. The building was deceptive because the basement let out at the back as a second story. The building facing the street contained offices and the front desk. The nefarious basement contained the holding cells and the medical examiner's office. Officers parked in a small parking lot and entered through the basement doors. Small but efficient, the Sheriff's office had not grown in a hundred years; no wonder, considering the low crime rate in such a small county.

      Sandra stood by the back door of the Sheriff's Office waiting for Ida and Jeff. The time was nearly an hour after midnight. Sandra just hoped no Sheriff's Deputy pulled into the parking lot, because she could not think of an excuse for being there. She kept glancing at the street light that illuminated the parking lot and made it obvious that someone was by the back door. She figured if there was ever a next time, she would shoot out the offending lamp with a BB gun.

      Jeff's car pulled into the parking lot. He honked the horn and waved with a big goofy grin on his face. Ida in the passenger seat just diverted her eyes. Both of them exited the vehicle and approached Sandra.

      "You want the whole town to know we are here?" asked Sandra.

      Jeff replied, "Relax. Billy is on duty tonight in the office, and he lost his hearing in World War whatever. Plus, Greg is out on patrol and won't be back until dawn."

      Jeff unlocked the back door and gestured for the girls to enter. After stepping through the door, Jeff turned on a light in the hallway. Luckily, no drunks were in the jail cells to the right, and the office's double doors for the medical examiners were held ajar by turn of the century spittoons.

      Paula lay on a metal slab in the middle of the room. Suddenly, Jeff did not feel like grinning anymore. He glanced at the girls and saw somber faces. He felt out of place and wondered what he was doing here. He trusted Sandra and Ida, but he had to admit it was spooky down in a basement with a body laid out in the middle of the room. He stood next to the door as the girls approached the body.

"Um, we may have a problem," said Sandra. "It looks like they have already drained the blood from the corpse."

"And why is that a problem?" asked Jeff. He looked at Sandra and Ida, who seemed confused. "And why do we need blood?"

Sandra pulled the silver knife from her back pack, and said, "Because we need to bathe the blade in blood for the ritual."

Jeff looked surprised, and said, "Listen, I thought you just wanted to see your friend. Not perform some kind of weird voodoo ritual."

Ida asked, "Jeff, did that thing in the alley seem normal to you?"

"Uh, no, not really."

"Well, the reason we are here is to perform a ritual on this knife to make it a terminal weapon."

"You mean make the knife into some kind of super knife. I did stab her, and she bled, so why do we need a super knife?"

Sandra replied, "It bleeds, but it will not die unless stabbed by a magical weapon."

"Okay, so you want to kill it," said Jeff.

Ida replied, "That is the only way to stop it."

Jeff stood there for a moment. He had known Sandra for most of his life. He knew she was a witch. The whole town knew she was a witch. He just never thought magic was real, but he thought what was in that alley was also not from any world he knew.

Jeff stood rooted to the spot next to the door, and asked, "Will an organ work?"

Sandra looked down at the knife and shrugged, saying, "Yeah, I guess if it is a liver or something."

Jeff did not move but pointed at some drawers on the far wall and said, "They keep the organs in there."

Ida wheeled a metal topped cart over to the drawers. She pulled on the handles, checking each drawer. Finally, she pulled a plastic bag out of one of the drawers with a liver in the bag. She placed the liver on the cart, and wheeled it into the middle of the room. She slid the liver out of the bag onto the cart.

Jeff watched them set up. First, Sandra pulled a compass out of her bag. Placing long tapered white candles around the liver, she used the compass to find true direction of North, East, West, and South. Sandra used a match to light the four candles. Sandra then pulled out of her bag a long, clear crystal attached to a string. She handed the crystal to Ida, and it fit completely in the crook of Ida's hand. Jeff felt nervous, but he could only watch, fascinated by the ritual.

Jeff saw Ida dangle the crystal over the liver. She swung the crystal like a pendulum. For some reason, he felt the palms of his hands sweating. He rubbed them on his thighs and continued to watch.

Sandra lifted the knife above her head, and said, "Bless this knife Hekate."

Jeff jumped as the flames on the table flared upwards a couple of inches. Jeff thought the room looked darker than a second ago. His stomach turned when Sandra stabbed the liver with the knife. Jeff heard Sandra and Ida chanting some nonsensical words. If they had meaning, Jeff could not tell.

Jeff wiped his eyes, because he swore the candle bases were turning red. A shiver went up his spine as he realized the candles were glowing red. Slowly, the candles seemed to wick blood from the liver into the candles' wax without actually touching the liver. The candles siphoned the blood of the liver turning the once white candles into dark red candles. Jeff's heart hammered in his chest. He looked at the girl's faces, and they were sweating.

Black smoke ballooned out of the liver. Jeff thought for a moment the candles had caught the liver on fire. He gasped as a discernable shape materialized in the smoke. The smoke was the face of Paula. Paula's smoky face screamed in a primordial rage for revenge. Jeff covered his ears.

Jeff saw eerie green light emanating from the crystal. The chanting grew louder. The chanting seemed to build into a crescendo. When the crystal popped, Jeff throttled his throat trying not to scream. Jeff let off a small moan when the candles flared, incinerating the blood red, wax candles in pillars of fire. The torches reminded Jeff of Lebanon. Bright lights with no discernable direction.

Jeff shook his head. Trying not to relive a terrible night in his past in Lebanon. He watched Sandra pull the blade from the liver. He chuckled, trying to relieve stress, as he noticed the blade had turned metallic red.

Sandra turned and said, "That's it."

Jeff replied, "Great, now let's get the fuck out of here."

Later that night, Jeff sat in his car at Ida's apartment complex. He had made small talk with Ida all the way back to her place. Not really saying anything, he just could not focus. He sat in the car, and could not remember what he had said when Ida opened the car door. He shook his head. He had to have said something, but he could not remember. He focused his attention on the steering wheel of the car. He could feel himself remembering. His eyes watered. He closed his eyes, and let the reel play in his head.

You could smell the heat. There was just no moisture in the air. Every day, the thermometer's mercury in the tube read over a hundred degrees Fahrenheit. The sun's rays beat down on your head like a sledge hammer. Waves of heat shimmered on the concrete pad. Dust clung to everything. The heat was the first impression of Lebanon. The second impression was the camp.

The camp housed twelve-hundred American Marines. Built on the back runway of the international airport in the western part of Beirut, the camp was surrounded by concrete structures to keep people and bullets out. Mortar nests, manned by Marines, were backed up against the wall. There were no towers for lookout posts. Just a concrete barrier to keep the men safe.

The Marines' task was security for the airport. In Beirut, there were three factions fighting for the heart of the city. One faction was the legitimate government of Lebanon. The other two factions had drawn a line in the sand. On one side the Christian faction, on the other side the Muslim faction, fought for control of the country. In the minds of the populace, the Marine camp had become a fourth faction. Americans were not to be trusted, so the Americans had become targets for the rage of the Christian and Muslim people.

The Marine camp was always on a heightened alert status. This was truly the first encounter of an American force dealing with a domestic, violent population. The Marines did not know who was friendly and who was foe. Around the camp, the people of Beirut walked around the city with RPGs strapped to their backs. Men carried automatic rifles over their shoulders. A fire fight could break out at any moment between the three factions of the city. The American Marine's high command ruled that unless fired upon, the Marines could not fire their weapons even as they watched men die literally twenty feet from the concrete barrier surrounding the camp. The constant vigilance took a toll on the Marines.

The American Marines had to remain alert against an attack. The heightened awareness emotionally stressed the Marines. At any moment, a mortar could be fired into the camp. The populace of the city would open fire on the Marines' concrete barricades. The city had become a conflict of death.

Jeff was assigned guard duty for the day at an entrance to the concrete barricade surrounding the camp. The constant pressure of watching the people mill around the airport heavily armed had worked its way into Jeff's soul. When would a shot ring out and kill him? Would it be that teenager carrying the RPG or the old man lumbering around with an AK-47 rifle. Jeff's fight was more ludicrous than he imagined. A sixteen-year-old boy lobbed a grenade close to Jeff's position. When the grenade exploded, the shrapnel killed a Marine ten feet away from Jeff. The shards of the grenade tore into Jeff's legs. He fell to the ground in agony. As he lay there bleeding, he could see the smile on the teenager's face.

When the reel stopped, Jeff took a solid breath. He jerked the gear shift into reverse, and peeled out of the parking lot. The reel was finished, so Jeff could feel a little peace for the immediate future.

Chapter Ten

The black Nissan pulled into a spot outside the Sheriff's office. Jeff sat for a moment. He stared at the entrance. His father had called him; leaving a cryptic message on his phone. He had been summoned by the all-powerful father figure. When Jeff had returned from overseas, back to this sleepy little town, he had spoken briefly to his father on the porch step of the family home. Jeff had not even bothered to go into the house. It felt more like a formality than a warm welcome home speech given by his father. They had never connected even when Jeff was young. Mike had always been the sheriff with all the rules, and the shallow expectations for Jeff to follow. As a child, Jeff wanted a father, not some parental figure head. Any subject broached, Jeff's father tried to make it a life lesson that a young man could never uphold. Not even deploying overseas in the Marines could stop his father from only speaking in platitudes about being a law-abiding citizen of the world. Jeff's father only cared about the next election, and how his son could fuck it up for him. His father cared more about the expectations of the town's people, than the expectations of his only son.

Life had been difficult with the father and son duo. Jeff's mother had died from lung cancer when Jeff was fourteen. Every day, Mike saw a little piece of his wife in Jeff. Mike missed her terribly, but never considered taking another wife. He poured all his energy into being the sheriff of a small county. He thought raising a son would be easy. He had guessed wrong.

Jeff sighed as he opened the door to the sheriff's office. Not much to it, the room housed three desks, and an enclosed office in the back. The front desk was manned by Billy. He was on the phone, but waved Jeff back to the office. The second desk was unmanned. Greg was out on patrol. The third desk remained empty, looking for an occupant. Jeff opened the door to his father's office.

"You're late," said Mike. "Sit down. I have to finish this paperwork."

Jeff sat in a chair in front of the desk. He looked around the office. Nothing had changed. A large bass mouth mounted behind the desk. A small head of a beaver Mike had trapped in Canada while hunting. Mike claimed the beaver saved him from starvation when he lost his compass in the wilds of Canada. Jeff knew the real reason the beaver was killed. It had the obvious problem of being cute.

"Pop, I don't have all day," said Jeff.

"Seems to me from what I hear, you do have all day," said Mike as he filed a couple pages in the desk drawer. "I hear you have been couch-surfing since you returned from the Marines. Why don't you find your own place? I mean, you are a grown man."

"I didn't come here for a lesson on how to be a man," said Jeff standing up.

"Whoa, just sit a moment," said Mike. "I have some serious questions to ask you about the murders in town. I hear your East Indian girl may be mixed up in it."

"Her name is Ida, and no, she isn't mixed up in anything."

"Listen, I don't care who you're dating or fucking, but we know the people involved with the past three murders are friends with Sandra and Ida. The FBI is breathing down my neck. They're talking about coming here. Here, dammit. In my town."

"Seems to me, the people are the town."

"Damn it Jeff, this is serious. The only reason I haven't pulled them in for questioning is because I've known Sandra for her complete life. I don't think she could be a part of this, but she does mess with some dark forces."

Jeff stared at him, and said, "What do you mean?"

"Well, those girls play grab ass in the middle of the woods during the full moon. Chanting or some shit. I'm not stupid. Witches have been a part of this town since the beginning. Most of the time, women just want to be heard, so they ask for things from Sandra. It's a bunch of bullshit; some people say she can do magic. All I know is we have a fingernail that is not human. That's right. It's from some kind of monster. Look, I've been the sheriff in this town for over thirty years. Some stuff, I just cannot explain. Especially to the fucking FBI. If something is happening then have Sandra tell me what the fuck it is so I can kill it."

"I don't know Pop, but I will talk to Ida and Sandra."

"Listen, there is another thing." Mike paused a moment. "You know there is an empty desk out there. I've been saving it for you. With your skills learned in the Marines, I think you could benefit the force. I know it isn't what you want, but just think about it. It's better than working some gas station."

"I'll think about it, and I will talk to Sandra and Ida," said Jeff.

"Well think about it, and get a fucking apartment. No son of mine needs to be a hippy."

Jeff stood up and turned his back on the old man. He thought, it will be a cold day in hell before I work for that man.

***

Jeff knocked on Ida's apartment door. He could hear her scrambling around the apartment and he grinned. He imagined her throwing clothes into a closet and a mountain of dishes piling up in the sink. Living alone does tend to be chaotic. You just lose interest in impressing yourself with a clean house.

Ida opened the door and smiled. She hesitated before kissing Jeff on the mouth. She just didn't know if their relationship expected anything else.

"Nice kiss, but can I come in?" asked Jeff.

Ida stepped aside and said, "Sure. Please don't mind the mess."

The apartment was a one bedroom and one bathroom rental. A little better than an efficiency apartment, but plenty of space for a single person. Jeff was a little surprised by the artwork on the walls. Most of them were actual paintings, not prints. The only consistency between all the paintings was some type of landscape. Mountains, woods, flowers, rivers, and a myriad of colors of nature's beauty. The apartment was sparsely furnished. A couch and a couple of chairs facing a wall with a large television. Two end tables and a coffee table rounded the room off.

"I'm surprised there are no plants," said Jeff.

"I've tried, but I just cannot keep them alive." She sat down in a chair, and motioned for Jeff to sit. She said, "I'm a little surprised myself that you dropped in unannounced. Please don't get me wrong. I loved that you came by. I mean," said Ida trailing the words off while blushing.

Embarrassed, Jeff said, "I didn't think about it. I mean, we are dating, right? I mean, we are past just hooking up."

Ida laughed, and then said, "I didn't mean to put you on the spot. And yes, I believe we are past just hooking up." Ida said coyly, "Unless, you came to hook up."

"That was the last thing on my mind." He stuttered, "I mean, I came by to talk to you about that thing that attacked us in the alley."

Ida laughed at his discomfort again, and said, "I guess we can actually talk instead of copulating." She put her hands in her lap, and said, "Ok, let's be serious."

"You're making fun of me now," said Jeff.

"Maybe, but would you like to talk now or …," asked Ida shyly.

The banter had heated Jeff up. Maybe she would be more forthcoming with information if she was more relaxed. Even Jeff thought that was a thin excuse to have sex, but Ida had a way of making Jeff horny. He just could not say no when she was ready to go.

After coitus, Jeff took a long drag from his cigarette. He was propped up against the headboard of Ida's bed. Jeff said, "You know, I think that was the best sex I have ever had."

Ida was nestled under his arm and replied, "Thank God you said that, because I could not keep up."

"By the way, I spoke to my father today. He believes the creature should be put down. Should we tell him what we know about the thing?"

Ida rolled over, and said, "If it was only the creature to deal with, then I would say yes. But, not only do we need to kill the thing, we also have to kill the mother who is a human being. I don't think your father would want to be a part of that even if the mother is as evil as the creature."

"Why kill the mother?"

"Because, she would not stop until she murdered everyone who participated in bringing that thing to justice."

"Justice meaning death."

"Are you afraid for me?"

"Absolutely! I mean that thing is dangerous."

"Well, I can be a little dangerous myself," said Ida. Even though she did not believe in what she just said to Jeff; the comment mollified him.

Chapter Eleven

The shack had been built in the late nineteenth century. It had been constructed to house a family of pickers on a cotton plantation. A string of five houses, only this one remained intact. The other's roofs had caved in or they had fallen off their rock foundations. Vagabonds had used the shacks for nearly a hundred years. Strewn debris was everywhere; things like tires, cans, and pieces of lumber littered the ground. The only thing of value was a water pump next to the shack. The pump's pipe, drilled into the earth ages ago, still produced water. A pipe sticking out of the ground with an S loop handle, the pump used a leather gasket to create a vacuum of air to pump water from an aquifer twenty feet below the surface. Ironically, the only way to use the pump was to prime it by pouring water down the pipe to saturate the leather gasket.

Parked beside the shack was an old rusted out blue Buick. Inside the shack, monsters had created a home. Vivian and Myra squatted in the one room house. Twenty feet square, the shack had loose wooden boards for a floor. In the corner, a pot belly wood stove provided heat in the winter and could be used as a cook top. Two sleeping bags were on one side, and clothes, strewn haphazardly, covered the floor. In another corner, a mound of fast-food bags smelled like rotten vegetables.

Vivian McDonnel lay on top of her bed roll. Gifted with a hundred years of agelessness by the satyr's lust, Vivian had squandered the privilege. Short, only five two, Vivian was lean. Her black hair, stringy and dirty, spread out on the pillow of the bed roll. Her left eye was missing. A cavity in a youthful face made her face even more sinister. Her nose had been broken several times over the years. Misshapen, her nose had a delicate smattering of brown freckles. When she smiled, people cringed. Her teeth were brown, and the roots were black. She bore keloid scars on her arms. In a pinch, she would cut herself to use her blood magic. At one time, she had been delicate and pretty, now her looks would scare any sensible person.

Vivian could hear Myra in the back of the shack feasting on some wild animal. As Myra tore the live animal apart, its pain filled screams haunted Vivian. Vivian feared Myra. Myra had become an unruly teenager while being physically eighty years old. A Grendel aged at a slower rate than a human. The first sixty years, Myra had been childlike with a child's need to impress her mother. Now, Myra had hit her puberty stage. A teenager could be deadly enough, because they do not understand what consequences are in this world, but a Faye creature that could live hundreds of years was primal and meant to live in the wilderness, not America's suburbia. It had to feed on live animals, including human beings. Vivian wondered if the monster in Myra would wake up one day and decide it did not need a mother.

The pump was making gurgling noises as it pumped water onto the ground. Myra was cleaning the blood off her naked body. She preferred to hunt nude. First, she washed her hands and arms. Then she splashed water on her pert breasts. Moving her hands between the cleavage of her breasts, she moved to her stomach wiping away the excess blood. Myra cupped her hands, and splashed water onto her supple thighs. Blood and water ran down her legs to her feet. Myra braced her arm on the side of the shack, and lifted each foot to wash off the last of the blood. Myra grabbed the S handle, and pumped it hard a couple more times before dunking her head under the spout cleaning her long red hair and face. She ducked again under the water spout, and greedily drank the cool water. Clean and satiated, Myra walked into the shack.

"Mother, I have a question." Myra grabbed a small sun dress off the floor and donned it. "Why did you stop me from ripping that Indian girl's throat out in the parking lot?"

Vivian rolled over in the makeshift bed to face Myra, and said, "As I have told you before, you can only attack someone in their home while they are alone. Do you want to spend a hundred years in a prison?"

"Prison. They would not be able to catch me."

"Well, they could catch me, and I don't want to spend a hundred years in a prison."

Myra laughed, and said, "You mean ten years in a prison. You will be dead soon, and then I will do what I want when I want."

Vivian lay flat, and said, "Yes, child. You will be able to do what you want when you want when I am dead, but first you must destroy this coven of witches."

Vivian's vendetta against the coven had only been a ruse. Decades ago, the coven had slighted Vivian. Now she was seeking revenge, and the thing called Myra had been begging to kill a human being. The situation was working for Vivian's benefit. The coven was slowly dying, and Myra would eventually be killed by the survivors of the coven. When Myra died, Vivian would finally be free from the responsibility of raising a monster. A monster with a teenager's temper that could strike out at any moment, ending Vivian's life. If the plan worked, she could then enjoy the last ten years of her enchanted life.

Unbeknownst to Vivian, Myra had her own plan. Myra had been ransacking the houses of the witches she had killed. She squirrelled away a number of pieces of jewelry. The plan was simple enough. Kill all the witches, take all the jewelry, and kill her mother when it was done. Only a pubescent teenager would not think of the consequences of her actions, only the grisly result. Teens vie for independence all the time, but only a monster would seek such a violent means to an end.

Chapter Twelve

As usual, Sandra was behind the counter of her store flipping through the latest magazine. She sat on a stool, unconsciously curling her toes and making the cheap, pink flipflops bang against her heel. The air conditioner worked, but on such a hot summer day, the store temperature inside topped seventy-eight degrees. To deal with the heat, she wore a pair of blue shorts snug against her thighs, and a white t shirt. Her long blonde hair, braided into a pony tail, hung down her back. She was dressed for the summer in the South Carolina heat.

The cow bell rang as a customer opened the door. It was a small town, so Sandra recognized Thelma even though she had never been in the store. Even in the heat, Thelma wore a dress to her knees with no cleavage showing. Thelma was the third-grade teacher at the local elementary school. Being in her late fifties, Thelma had taught Sandra how to read in school. Everyone in town knew Thelma to be a strait-laced, practical person. Sandra could not imagine why Thelma had decided to come into her shop.

"Hi, Thelma. Can I help you?" asked Sandra.

Looking a little bit nervous, Thelma replied, "Yes, dear. I came about a simple matter. Can we talk?"

Sandra slid off the stool, and came around the counter, "Anything for you. You know, you taught me the ABC sing song."

Thelma laughed, "I seem to remember you drove the lunch women mad, because you kept repeating the song over and over again during lunch."

"Well, it seemed important."

"Any who, I came to talk to you about a delicate manner."

"Trust me. Anything you say will stay with me."

"Well, I, uh." She stopped for a moment, and then hurriedly said, "I have a small problem with my husband. We want to, you know, but he has problems. Jesse said you could fix it."

"His lead pipe is not quite as full?"

Thelma placed her hand over her mouth, and her eyes brightened. She just nodded at Sandra.

"Give me a couple of minutes. I just got in a new batch of magazines. Take a look around, while I go to my apartment above the store."

Thelma smiled, and nodded acquiescence.

Thelma watched Sandra go upstairs, then walked over to the magazine rack. She was a little surprised at the variety of magazines, and then she saw "Garden Plus", a magazine she could not find anywhere else in town. She always had to go to the Columbia mall to find it. She decided maybe the store was not as bad as some had deemed it. Besides, she had known Sandra for years. She should have come in the store years ago. She grabbed the magazine, and decided to purchase it.

Sandra came down the stairs with her flipflops flopping. She went behind the counter. She punched in twenty dollars and three dollars for the magazine.

"Your total today is twenty-three dollars," said Sandra, smiling at Thelma. She reached down and grabbed a bag. She put the magazine and a small vial into the bag.

Thelma gave her exact change.

"Ok," said Sandra. "There are thirty drops in the vial. You want to mix three drops into liquid. Just don't put it in alcohol or fruit juices. The vial is good for ten doses. Then wait about ten minutes after he drinks the liquid."

Thelma grabbed the bag and said, "Three drops and ten minutes. Got it."

Thelma started for the door as Ida walked in. They nodded at each other as they passed in the doorway. Ida wore a white and pink sundress. The dress was white with a pattern of pink roses. The dress came to mid-thigh, and her shoes were white strappy sandals. The dress had a large cleavage shaped like a U. Her brown breasts seemed to burst from the dress, and her breasts glistened from the hot summer day.

"Glad to see you made a sale," said Ida.

Sandra smiled and said, "I think she is going to be a regular. Listen, I don't want you to be frightened but I followed you and Jeff a couple nights ago."

Ida laughed, and said, "Looking for pointers?"

"Very funny. No. I had a hunch that thing may have been pissed off about being stabbed."

"And?"

"I saw it in the parking lot with the blood witch."

"Crap. You think Jeff is in danger?"

"I don't know, but I am giving the knife to you. It may come back."

"What do I do if it comes back?"

Sandra smiled, and said, "Stab it silly girl."

"Seriously. I don't know if I could do it."

Sandra placed her hands on both shoulders of Ida, and replied, "You are a Nature Witch. We deal with supernatural things all the time. Do not worry. You can protect yourself. I believe in you."

Ida slowly breathed out, and said, "Ok."

Sandra walked away and sat back on her stool behind the counter. She said, "By the way, you seem to be seeing a lot of Jeff lately."

A coy smile graced Ida's lip. "Yeah, we have become friendly."

"Good. I need you to ask him a favor."

"The last time I asked him for a favor we ended up in the sack."

"Like you would mind. So," Sandra passed a sheet of paper to Ida. "Here is the plate number on the blue Buick. See if he can find out who owns the car, and maybe we can get ahead of this thing."

"Got it."

Ida glanced at the paper, and hoped this would lead them to the blood witch. Her friends were dying. She resolved that she would personally see the end of that terrible monster and the creature's mother. She figured the world would just be a better place.

Chapter Thirteen

Ida and Jeff lay naked on top of the cover and sheets of the bed. Both of them were drenched in sweat from the heavy love making on a hot summer's day. Ida's head, tucked under Jeff's arm and laying on his chest, made Jeff smile. He had never clicked with someone on the deepest level while having sex as much as he had with Ida. The sex was mutual give and take, and both of them gave as much as they would take. He had feelings for Ida, but the sex was pure animalistic lust between two young people. He had been in love with just one other girl in his life, but the sex did not compare to this union. His dalliances with other women in his adult life seemed trivial now.

"Penny for your thoughts?" asked Ida.

"You do not want to know my thoughts."

"Try me," she said, nuzzling his hairy chest.

"How do I put it. I mean, the sex is great, but it's not just that. I mean, I have never felt so alive."

"I understand," Ida replied. "I feel the same way. I am not going to back you in a corner and say you must love me. I do have feelings. I just don't know what they are at the moment. I think we should just enjoy it. We just have to let our feelings percolate."

"Thank you. Not just for that, but for not trying to back me in a corner. I enjoy being with you, not just for the sex, but in everything else as well."

Ida squeezed his chest and said, "Let's just enjoy this for a while, then revisit our feelings later. Do you want a glass of tea? I'm dying of thirst."

Jeff laughed, and said, "God, yes."

Ida got out of bed. Her nubile body was perfect. Her sensual walk out of the bedroom thrilled Jeff. She came back a couple of minutes later holding two glasses of sweet tea. She sat on the edge of the bed, and handed one of the glasses to Jeff.

Ida said, "I have another favor to ask."

Jeff sat up in bed and said, "The last time you asked a favor, I saw some weird shit."

"You mean magic."

Jeff drank half the glass of tea to quench his thirst, and then said, "Yeah, about that. Is magic always that scary?"

Ida laughed, and said, "Goddess, no. Nature magic is communing with people and the wilderness. It's true, some magic is dangerous. You saw a ritual that I hope I will never do in this life again, but in all things, there is dark and there is light. Nature magic is usually the light, but sometimes Nature Witches move in the shadows. Now, a Blood Witch like the one we are fighting thinks only of the power you can get from magic. Being a solitary witch, she will never feel the communion of a coven. The love for one another."

"So, you are in love?"

"Silly. Of course, but not love like between a man and a woman. Think of it as more a parental love shared by the coven."

"That seems slightly incestuous."

"Have you ever had sex with a girl who was a dear friend first?"

"Yes."

"Well, think of it that way. You loved her as a friend, but you were not *in* love with her."

Jeff smiled, "I think I understand. Anyway, what is this favor?"

"We got the license plate number of the blood witch."

"Um, Ok, but I can't just walk in the police station and say, hey, give me a name."

"Yeah, I really hadn't thought of that. What can you do?"

"Let me think about it for a minute," said Jeff. They both sipped their tea. Both of them were trying to think of a solution.

"I think I've got it," said Jeff. "It would be a small favor. I wouldn't even have to ask my father. I'll just tell them she scratched my car in a parking lot, and I need her insurance information to fix it."

"Brilliant. Ok, now that we have hydrated, let's have round two."

Chapter Fourteen

Mary Quarles' show was coming on tonight. Like every Wednesday night, Mary made dinner. She liked cooking. She was actually better than average with her culinary skills, but she never cooked for anyone else. She never had a father after he left her mother when Mary turned five. Her mother before she died said a good cook makes a good wife. Maybe from her mother's meddling or her father's death, Mary lived a lonely life.

Mary did not miss her mother. She had been full of platitudes and drama. Mary often dragged her to bed after her mother drank a pint of vodka. With the whole house to herself after her mother passed out, usually around ten o'clock at night, Mary would perform magic in her bedroom. She liked pyrokinesis. The flames she created came in multiple forms and colors. She never lost control of the flame. She could manipulate fire in multiple forms. Angry, red fire, yellow, soothing fire, and the happy, blue flames were her friends. She could create flaming orbs, blankets of fire, and streams that seemed to evaporate out at the end. She could create bursts of fire like the Fourth of July fireworks you see in the sky. The conflagrations never left the palm of her cupped hands. It was more about manipulating the fire in her hands than making a weapon that could hurt someone. Like her cooking, she did not share this talent with anyone.

Her show was on. She liked the cop's attitudes, and the bad guy always getting caught for any dastardly deed. She sat on the couch curled up with a bowl of popcorn every week. She was always alone except on this special night.

Myra was annoyed. The only way into Mary's home was the bathroom window. Mary had not bothered to lock it because the window was so small. It was a round, decorative window only thirty-two inches wide. Myra had pulled a Houdini. She had to dislocate her shoulder to fit through the window. It was more uncomfortable than actually hurting. The shoulder unnaturally popped back into place. No, the annoyance came from climbing through the window upside down hanging onto a clothes basket for balance. Myra just felt undignified.

Myra crept to the bathroom door. Opening it to peek out, she could hear the television. Making her way down the hallway, she could hear Mary laugh at some scripted joke on the show. Myra decided to scare the living shit out of Mary. She would jump out of the doorway to the living room, and yell out.

Myra jumped and yelled, "Boo!" For her effort, sparks lit up in front of her face. The fire burned her eyebrows. She had to rub the flames out with the palms of her hands. Now she was not irritated, but angry. She screamed like a banshee and ran for Mary. Mary had by then reached the other side of the room into the hallway. Myra followed, never letting the unearthly scream reach a peak. She turned a corner and saw Mary fling salt onto the door seal of an adjoining room. Running at full speed, Myra slammed into an invisible barrier made of air. Her nose snapped, and she bounced against the barrier falling down backwards. Laying on her back, she was not angry. Her anger blossomed into rage. She jumped up and kicked and punched the barrier with her feet and hands. Blood and slobber clung to the barrier in midair and her mouth frothed. After railing on the barrier for several minutes, Myra stopped and stared at her trapped quarry.

"I know what you are thinking. Will the barrier last or will it fall," said Mary. She just smiled.

"What was that thing you threw at my face? The sparks," asked Myra.

"Just friends of mine."

"Well, it burned off my eyebrows, so I think I will eat your eyes first."

Mary laughed. The longer she laughed, the more scared she became that she would not be able to stop laughing. After a couple of minutes, the laugh subsided. Wiping tears from her eyes, she stared at Myra for a moment. This creature of no remorse stared back.

"I don't know why you are laughing," said Myra. "But you are going to die."

"Maybe, but not tonight. You see, this is my sanctum. As long as I live, the barrier won't come down."

"Now it is my turn to laugh, because you are trapped and I can wait much longer than you can. Eventually, you would starve to death."

"Children always cannot see out of a box." With a flourish, she raised a telephone. "Should I call the police, or my fellow witches?"

Myra stared at her hard for a minute, and then answered, "Another day then, but I promise you it will be painful."

"Expect no less from me," whispered Mary.

Chapter Fifteen

The stars in the sky seemed to extend into the universe. The quarter moon was a sliver in the sky. No city light penetrated the night. The coven stood in a circle around a firepit in a field. The firepit's coals were cold. Tonight, the witches did not celebrate any black sabbath. Tonight, plans would be drawn to defeat the Blood Witch and the monster.

Each witch offered a prayer to their favorite deity in silence. Wearing a loose fit black robe with a hood, the witches waited patiently for Sandra to speak. The wind stirred the bottom of the robes. The ripple of wind exposed the witches' bare feet. Tonight, the summer heat did not bother them. All of them were naked under the cotton robes.

"I have called the coven to discuss how we may defeat the killers," said Sandra Laughlin.

Henry Stapper asked, "There's more than one?"

Sandra replied, "As you know, there is a Faye creature stalking us. Also, a Blood Witch is controlling it. From what I have gathered, the Blood Witch is its mother. I saw them together watching Ida outside of the Conservatory."

Mary Quarles spoke up, which was unusual for her. "It is a nasty thing full of hate and venom."

Ida Makmur replied, "I'm just glad you survived the attack."

All the witches murmured their heartfelt agreement.

"So, what's the plan?" asked Natalie Alkaev. "We just can't let it come to us. Mary was fortunate. This thing sounds like a beast."

"We do have a weapon," said Sandra. "But we only have one cursed knife."

Linda Magetti said, "We have to keep it out of our homes. It seems it only attacks us inside our homes."

"Do we know anything?" asked Kelly Brook.

Sandra replied, "I think we are safe in the world, but you're right. Maybe, it understands it can be caught if seen. We all live alone."

"So, what, do we take a long vacation, or do we kill it?" retorted Kelly Brook.

"Don't forget the Blood Witch. She will turn on us if we kill her prodigy," said Sally' Ann O'Conner.

"Listen. I think the Blood Witch is letting her do the work. After we destroy it, she will come for us, but one thing at a time," replied Linda Magetti.

"We need something to protect us," said Henry.

"I may have a short-term solution," said Muriel Stamos. "We need a ward to keep it out of our homes."

"That would have to be a powerful ward to keep the Faye out," said Kelly.

"Maybe we should talk to the Fairies," said Natalie Alkaev. "In Russia, Fairy wards are powerful."

"But are they here?" asked Henry.

"Yes, we have Fairies here," replied Sandra. "They are in the hills and mountains of upper South Carolina. The question is whether they will talk to us."

Natalie asked, "Do we need to make an offering?"

Ida spoke, "No, but the timing has to be right. I once read a book about Fairies. During a clear night, they congregate on a circle of toadstools at midnight."

"That's helpful," said Kelly sarcastically.

"We need a ward," said Sandra. "Ida and I will go to the hills and find the Fairies."

"What do we do in the meantime?" asked Henry.

Sandra replied, "We bunk up. No one should be alone during the night."

"Simple solution, but what about the Blood Witch?" asked Mary. "Even after we put the ward in place, she could circumvent it."

Ida replied, "Jeff is working on that. He is going to find out who the Blood Witch is. She is not immune to our magic like the Faye. If we have to. We can curse her."

The group grumbled.

Henry replied, "Curses have a way of coming back on the witch that casts the spell."

Ida replied, "We just need to slow the witch down, not kill her."

Muriel Stamos replied, "I have a spell. I once used it in my youth to punish a rival during high school. It is not much, but shitting yourself constantly can be distracting. I just need something tangible to focus it on the Blood Witch."

"We will try to find something," replied Sandra. "In the meantime, stay together until we talk to the Fairies."

"Wait," said Kelly. "What about Paula's funeral? I haven't heard anything."

Sandra replied, "She left special instructions in her will. She made me the executer. I cremated her and scattered her ashes in the Edisto River."

Natalie replied, "Edisto River, huh. I'm not surprised. Everyone here has been in that rickety old canoe."

The coven murmured agreement.

Sandra replied, "That is what she wanted. Now, stay safe, and pair up."

All of them agreed. Each of them knew they were talking about life and death. This monster was killing them one by one, but meddling with forces of nature was part of being a witch.

As the group walked back to their cars, they paired off, making arrangements on who would stay with whom. All the cars were parked on a dirt road next to the field. Being of red clay, the road seemed to be an orange river running beside the fields. After years of scraping, the road even had banks like a river bed.

Ida and Sandra watched the cars leave one at a time.

"You think we can find the Fairies up north?" asked Sandra.

Ida replied, "It shouldn't be a problem finding the toadstools. I can make a divining rod that will lead us to Fairy magic. I do see two problems. One, the meeting places of Fairies are normally deep in the woods, and two, they may not even bother to materialize to be spoken to."

"Well, don't worry about getting lost in the woods. I have a couple of spells that can lead us out. The Fairies are finicky though. We may have to come back several nights in a row."

"Sounds like a camping trip."

"Yeah, well, you may need to talk to your beau about being gone for several days."

Ida laughed, and said, "I just hope he is my beau. We are kind of in a weird place right now."

"Weird good, or weird bad?"

"I think we are good."

Sandra just nodded. She looked up at the moon, and wondered if it would be full before they talked to the Fairies. Sandra took a deep breath of the night air. She did not mind a couple of days in the deep wood. She liked the peace and tranquility of the woods. Besides, beer next to a fire would calm her nerves, and her nerves needed to be calmed after the past month of death.

Chapter Sixteen

The couple's bliss from copulating had completely relaxed them. As usual, Ida's head rested on Jeff's chest. Jeff's hair was mussed from Ida's excited hair pulls during love making. His lean body was completely relaxed. The taut muscles normally disguised his unusual strength. His stomach, flat and muscled, quivered from the strenuous exercise of sex. His penis, placid now, had been full and erect during sex. The only thing marring the buff body was the irregular scars on his thighs and shins. The grenade had tagged him for life.

"You know, I came over to talk," said Jeff.

"Maybe, but I do not know when we will be able to do this again," replied Ida. "Sandra and I are going on a camping trip to the foothills of the Blue Ridge Mountains."

"Does it have to do with that monster?"

"You worry too much. We will be perfectly fine. We are just going to talk to some Fairies."

"I don't know why we just can't shoot this thing."

"It is a being of magic. Bullets will not affect it. The gun would slow it down, but the healing qualities of being a Grendel means it won't die. Only a magic weapon can kill it. That is why we have the knife."

"So, what is in the mountains?"

"We are hoping the Fairies can help us keep the damn thing out of our homes."

"I like that idea."

"You won't like this one. Until it is dead, each of the coven is bunking up with each other, so unless you can get a place by the time, I get back we're on a sabbatical."

"Yeah, I've been thinking about that. My savings are starting to get low. I need to find a job."

"Doing what?"

"I don't really know. It is a small town. I might have to drive to Columbia to get a job. My father offered me a job as a cop, but I don't know if I can work with him."

"Because he's difficult to work with, or you just have history?"

"A little of both, but being a cop does appeal to me. My training as a Marine could come in handy, and I like helping people."

"Well, that's it. Take the job. It's not like you can't quit if you don't like it. He's the public servant, and you would just be an employee."

"I'll think about it. So, how long will you be gone?"

"Miss me already?" asked Ida with a smile.

Jeff laughed, "Yeah, I miss you all ready."

"Well, I was packing before you got here. By the way, did you run down that tag number?"

"I talked to Billy. He said to give him a couple days, but he'll have it."

"Great. Now, silly, get out of my bed so I can pack."

"Do you need help?"

"No. Sandra should be here in about half an hour, so first, I need to take a shower." Ida kissed Jeff on the mouth, and said, "I will miss this for the next couple of days."

Jeff reached for his shirt and said, "Yeah, me too."

As Jeff dressed himself, Ida stepped into the shower. Humming a soft tune, Ida washed her hair and body. She stepped over the tub lip, and grabbed a towel. She heard Jeff in the other room.

"Not gone yet?"

"Ow, he is gone," said Myra. "He locked the door behind him, and I had to force it open."

Ida dropped the towel and moved down the hallway to the living room. She hoped her naked body would distract the monster.

Myra smacked her lips, and said, "You look delicious. I don't think I've ever had East Indian take out before."

Myra was lounging on the couch between Ida and her purse. The knife was in the purse hanging by the door.

"I would have straightened up if I had known company was coming over."

Myra smiled and said, "Yeah, I could hear the company all the way down the stairs."

"So, you were waiting for Jeff to leave?"

"Yeah, well, I wanted dinner, and he could be bothersome."

Ida moved towards the door.

"Are you really trying to escape? I mean, what, you're just going to run down the stairs butt-naked?"

"No. I just figured a little lip stick, so that when I die, I will have just a little bit of makeup on."

"Oh, don't worry. I plan on taking time with you. When I'm finished, your own mother won't recognize you."

Ida pulled the Venetian blade from her purse, "I don't think you will have the time."

"Huh, a knife. I must say it is kind of long. When I take it from you, I think I will stab you in the eye with it."

Myra stood up from the couch. With a twisted smile on her face, she moved closer to Ida. Ida stood between her and the door.

Myra paused and said, "I smell magic."

Ida lunged at Myra with the knife. Myra raised her left hand to protect her face. The blade stabbed her in the palm. A stream of black smoke burst from the wound. The pain was excruciating. Myra raised her chin and screamed. The crease in her head opened like a flower and trumpeted a high note. The crease was not a third eye. It was a third orifice on her face. Two holes with a slit down the middle, the hole could smell the magic in the knife. Myra, holding her hand, ran out the door.

Myra stumbled to the blue Buick in the parking lot. She opened the door with her uninjured hand, and cried out, "Mama, the bitch stabbed me with a magic knife."

"Get in," shouted Vivian. Vivian peeled out of the parking lot. She drove at high speed to reach the cabin in the woods. Myra rotated between a moan and a scream the entire trip.

Vivian's plan was unraveling. She had thought she wanted the creature dead, but as a mother, she wanted her daughter to live.

The drive to the cabin took ten minutes. Vivian had blown every stop sign and traffic light. She had passed cars on the double yellow line. She worried it could be too late. A magic knife could have ill effects on the Faye.

Vivian rushed Myra into the cabin. She threw coal on the fire to bank the heat in the pot stove.

"Let me see it," said Vivian.

Crying, Myra held out her hand. The wound was a putrid black hole. Puss ran out in a steady stream.

"It's definitely magical in nature," said Vivian.

Myra moaned, "Can you stop the pain?"

"Yes, but you will lose the hand."

Myra shook her head violently, and screamed, "No! No!"

"It's the only way to stop the infection." Vivian grabbed the iron poker, and drove the tip into the hot coals of the pot stove. "I just hope we are not too late. Give me a minute while the poker heats."

Vivian ran out the door. She opened the trunk of the car and grabbed a machete. She tested the edge. Not exactly sharp, but it would have to do. She ran back into the cabin. Grabbing the iron poker, she checked the heat. It was glowing slightly red. She stuck it back into the fire.

"Come here girl," said Vivian.

Myra shook her head no.

Looking directly into Myra's eyes, she repeated, "Come here girl."

Crying. Myra slowly walked over to her mother.

"Stand next to the stove, and put your finger tips on the top. Leave your left hand on the stove, and extend your arm away from you parallel to the floor."

Vivian eyed the wrist. It was not particularly thick, but she knew it was held together with small bones. She could not imagine taking a second swing, so the first one must be fast and hard. She could see Myra staring at her with tears running down her cheeks. Vivian could not hesitate. She raised the machete over her head, took a big breath and held it. She slammed the machete down on the wrist as hard and fast as she could with one blow. The wrist parted. The hand lay on top of the stove, and Myra grabbed her arm and screamed, she trumpeted out of her forehead. With each heartbeat, a spurt of blood from the bloody stump hit the floor.

Vivian grabbed the poker out of the fire. She did not say a word. Walking calmly over to Myra, Vivian wrenched Myra's arm down. Vivian shoved the poker into the bloody wound. The smell of burning flesh filled the room. Myra trumpeted again, then promptly fainted. She fell face first onto the floor.

Vivian walked over to the stove to check the hand. The rot had not set into the base of the hand. The palm was black and meaty. Vivian figured she had severed the hand in time before the magic had spread. If the stab wound had been on her person, Myra would not have survived. Vivian figured she had another reason to kill those witches. No one should hurt her child. She gently picked up the hand by the thumb, and tossed the blackened hand into the fire.

Chapter Seventeen

The VW Bug sounded like angry crickets had made a nest in the back of the car. Sandra and Ida were on the road. Sandra preferred the back roads to the mountains. On the interstate, big trucks would push the Bug all over the road. The high speeds put a strain on the engine, and Sandra worried her precious Bug could not take the heat. Besides, the small towns on the backroads were interesting. Quaint red brick downtowns in the heart of nowhere appealed to Sandra.

"We're coming up to a gas station on the right. Time for a pit stop," said Sandra. "She needs to be gassed up."

Sandra pulled the Bug over, and lined up with the pumps. Both of them hopped out. They looked almost identical. Both of them wore tight white t-shirts and khaki cargo shorts. For the hike ahead, both of them had bought ankle high, brown hiking boots from a shoe store in downtown Clear View. Ida headed for the gas station to pay for the gas and snacks. Sandra filled up the tank.

As Ida exited the gas station door, a pick-up truck turned into the parking lot. Painted white and red, the truck had seen better days. Sores of rust covered the truck. The driver, grinning at both of them, showed his yellow teeth stained from years of smoking. He wore a dirty baseball cap with an indistinguishable logo.

The truck driver slapped the door panel outside of the truck to get the girls attention and said, "Ooh, baby. I would pay full price for you, but half for your friend. Where ya'll headed? You could come with me if you like."

Ida just ignored him and slid in the passenger seat. Sandra, on the other hand, gave him the middle finger as she climbed into the driver's seat.

As she pulled out of the parking lot, Sandra checked her rear-view mirror to see if the truck was following them. She need not have worried though, the truck driver pulled out of the gas station headed the opposite way.

"Colorful people in the South," commented Ida.

"Yeah, there are assholes everywhere," replied Sandra.

Small little towns gave way to strands of trees. Even on a hot summer day, both of them rolled down the windows. You could smell pine trees in the air. Even though the land had been logged out ages ago, the trees and underbrush had rebounded in this protected forest. Shadows from the trees played on the windshield of the car.

"OK, we made it to mother earth. Where to now?" asked Ida.

"We can set up on a primitive campsite in the National Forest. I think our best bet is Ellicott Rock Wilderness. It's on the southern part of the Blue Ridge Mountains in South Carolina. There are some trails, but we can easily go off trail."

As the car slowly wound its way through the forest on a black top road, both of them enjoyed the tranquility of the park. After driving for half an hour in the vibrant green foliage, Sandra saw a sign for Ellicot Rock Wilderness camp sites. She turned right onto a dirt road. Up ahead was a small, one room hut sitting in the middle of the road guarding the lanes coming in and out of the forest. You passed on the right of the building to enter. Sandra drove up to the building's right side where a woman leaned out the window.

"How can I help you?" asked the woman. She wore a brown ranger's hat.

Sandra replied, "We want a primitive campsite."

"Let me check the map. You're in luck, we have a site that is open for the next three days. It's kind of far from the utility building, but this time of year you're lucky it's open."

"How much is it?"

"Twelve dollars a night. Paid in advance."

Sandra glanced at Ida. Ida nodded.

"We'll take all three nights," replied Sandra.

"Looky here. This forest is a pack in and pack out site. No trash in my forest. Got it?"

Sandra smiled and said, "No problem, ma'am."

Sandra settled the bill. The woman handed her a childlike map of the campsites. The site circled with a pen was for thirty-six on the map. Sandra followed the map down dirt roads to their campsite. They found a break in the road to the right where three cars were parked. Sandra pulled into the last spot. A small wooden sign on the side of a dirt trail was labeled with the numbers of the sites. Sandra and Ida grabbed their equipment and walked down the path. The sites were spaced out about every fifty yards. They smiled and waved at people as they passed the sites on the trail. Coming to an end, a small sign in the dirt said thirty-six. It was basically a small clearing on the side of the trail.

"What do we do if we have to pee?" asked Ida.

Sandra laughed, and said, "You just have to let it hang out, but avoid any bush with triangular leaves."

They set up the tent for the night.

After setting up the tent and camping chairs around the cold fire pit, they ate a dinner of trail mix and some candy bars, then they discussed their next move.

"So, what do you have?" asked Sandra.

"It's a divining rod." Ida pulled a small Y shaped tree branch out of a bag. "You hold the ends with both hands and the tip dips when you are going in the right direction, but it doesn't follow paths, so we'll have to tramp our way through the undergrowth to find a circle of magic toad stools. So, how do we get back?"

"Ah-ha," Sandra replied. "My grandmother's finder kit." She reached into her bag and retrieved a couple of wire coat hangers cut and shaped like an L. She also pulled out a man's wrist watch. "Well, my grandfather was known to get drunk and fall down somewhere in town." She stood up and placed the wrist watch on a rock near the entrance of the camp. She walked back and sat in the chair. Holding the wire in each hand straight out, she said, "See, you hold a wire in each hand with the long parts sticking out over the top of your hands. Keeping your hands a few inches apart, the wires are pointing forward, but when they are pointed in the direction of the watch, they cross." She demonstrated by moving her outstretched arms in the direction of the watch on the rock. As soon as the wires were in a direct line to the watch, they crossed each other like an X. "Magic."

"You know, this would be a lot easier if either one of us could use a compass in the woods," said Ida.

"Now that would be a good skill to have, but this will have to do. I say we take an hour nap, and when it gets dark, we set out."

"Agreed. Let's put the flash lights on the chairs, so we can find them in the dark."

Sandra climbed on all fours to enter the tent. Ida scrambled in after her. Before lying on the bedrolls, they kissed each other good night. As the sun slowly set, both of them fell asleep.

Later that night, an owl high in a tree hooted. Three short blasts, and one long one. The noise woke Sandra. She had been sleeping soundly after the long car ride. She checked her watch. It was ten thirty at night. Ida slept on her back, softly snoring. Sandra hated to wake her up, but it was time to go. They both crawled out of the tent. Ida found the flashlights and Sandra gathered up a couple of water bottles for the hike. She put the bottles, some trail mix, and the finder kit in a backpack.

"Ready to go?" asked Sandra.

"Yeah, but which way should we go? We need to find a clearing in the woods with toad stools. It won't be near a trail."

"Yes. I was thinking we start on a trail that leads to the deep woods. Here, look at the campsite map. As you can see in the back of the campsites, a hiking trail leads to a small waterfall about a mile up. I say we start there, then use the wand until it takes us off trail."

"Well, it's a plan. Let's go."

Both of them turned on the flashlights and headed towards the car. As they passed the other sites, one reeked of marijuana, one couple sat around a fire and waved as they passed, and in the third one you could hear and see the silhouette of two men having sex in a tent. When they reached the car, they turned down a dirt road headed to the back of the park towards the forest.

"Here's the trail," said Ida. The flashlight lit a sign set next to the trail head. The sign showed a curvy route to the falls. An easy hike, if you stayed on the trail. They nodded to each other and walked into the forest at night.

The flashlights cut the night like a knife. The beams of light seemed to make the wide, easy trail a thing to be feared. Things scurried from the light. Branches swayed with the slight wind. The clouds hid the moon. Both of them were wide-eyed, trying to see past the light. The path was easy to walk, so it took them thirty minutes to reach the falls.

Ida grabbed the divining rod. Holding on to it and the flashlight, she turned around in a small circle. It dipped, pointing off the trail to the right of the waterfall. They had to walk through a steady stream of water over gray, round rocks. Past that point, the forest seemed like a dark wall made of trees and brush. Ida pushed her way into the woods.

The forest undergrowth pulled at their exposed legs. After walking in a straight line for about a hundred yards, they came upon a small cliff in the middle of the forest. The divining rod pointed over the side of the cliff. Instead of climbing down and risk falling, they walked a parallel course; keeping the cliff on their right-hand side. After a few yards, the ground sloped down to a small stream of water that had fashioned the cliff over time. Both of them jumped the course of water to the other bank. Taking out the divining rod, Ida motioned in the dark. Sandra felt a little creepy watching Ida's back in the small circle of the flashlight. After walking through the forest for about half an hour, Ida's circle of light spotted a ring of mushrooms near two large trees.

"I think this is it," said Ida.

"How do you know so much about fairies?" asked Sandra.

Ida propped the rod against a tree, then sat down next to it, and replied, "It was kind of a hobby while I was in college. I liked all the drawings in old books about fairies. Most of it was hogwash, but I believe some of it to be true. Now, we have to wait until midnight. We have to be still and quiet. The fairies will show themselves only if they deem to."

Sandra checked her watch, thirty minutes until midnight. She sat down next to Ida. Both of them just stared at the ring of mushrooms trying not to feel silly. Sandra had seen many manifestations of magic, but had never seen one of the Faye. She waited in the dark for one of earth's eldest creatures.

In the center of the ring of mushrooms, a tiny lantern appeared. The light from the lantern pushed the dark night out. The light was so bright that the circle of mushrooms interfered with the light, casting long shadows on the ground. The circle was perfectly lit.

On the largest mushroom, a naked fairy materialized out of thin air. The wings looked like a dragon fly. The gossamer wings fluttered as the delicate fairy with white blond hair sat cross-legged on the top of the mushroom. Barely an inch high, she spread her small arms out beckoning the other fairies to appear. Slowly, one by one, fairies found a roost on the mushrooms. Three male fairies with genitalia protruding from their pelvises smiled at the humans and then sat down on the edge of the mushrooms, dangling their feet. Four female fairies, all with shockingly bright red hair, puffed into existence on the other mushrooms. Flapping their wings, the females' breasts bounced like small waves. A chorus of high pitch whines and whistles permeated the air as they talked amongst themselves. After a minute, the first fairy that had appeared whistled. The fairies settled down. Obviously, the blonde-haired fairy that had appeared first was the queen.

Ida whispered, "We came here to seek advice."

"What advice do you seek?" asked the blonde fairy.

"We wish to stop a creature from entering our homes, and murdering us in our sleep."

All the fairies' wings buzzed. The clicks and whistles chimed again. The blonde raised her hand. They stopped talking amongst themselves.

The blonde fairy asked, "Is it a creature of the Night People or one of the Faye?"

"It is a Grendel."

All the wings buzzed at once, and the fairies became excited. Chirping the loudest was one of the red-haired fairies.

The blonde fairy spoke to Ida. "We can give you a ward to stop the Grendel from entering your home, but we need to trade."

"What could a fairy want?"

"We wish for you to kill a rabid vampire."

Ida looked at Sandra and shrugged. Ida had never seen a vampire.

Sandra asked, "Aren't vampires' part of the forest? Why would you want to kill one of the vampire clan's own?"

"This vampire does not have a clan. It has become rabid. The local clan of vampires have banished him. He was killing without feeding. He has eaten three of my fairy brood."

Ida looked at Sandra with a question in her eyes. Sandra just nodded ascent.

Sandra replied, "I do not condone killing one of the Night People without cause, but a murdering vampire must go."

"Nila will lead you to the vampire. She is very brave." One of the red-haired fairies preened. Glancing over to the small fairy, the blonde fairy continued, "She lost a sister to the vampire. Her grief is so great that she will lead you to the vampire during the day. Go back to your camp, and at noon, she will appear. After the deed has been done, she will give you the secret to the ward that will stop a Grendel, and she will give you this."

One of the male fairies shook a tiny leather flagon.

"In the flagon are the tears of my kind gathered after the death of our sisters and daughters rendered by the rabid vampire. It will aid you in creating a powerful ward."

A small breeze extinguished the lamp. The fairies disappeared.

"What do you know about vampires?" asked Ida.

"Enough to know we do not want to be in these woods for very long. Let's get moving. I will tell you about vampires when we get back to camp."

Chapter Eighteen

In the early morning sun, the squat brick building cast a shadow on the sidewalk. The jailhouse, built of red brick with rebar on the windows, was the county home for the Sheriff's Department. Old men passed the building while walking on the sidewalk to Sally's Kitchen. Sally's Kitchen eked out an existence catering to old men and their coffee in the early morning light. Not one old man bothered to peer into the windows of the jailhouse. Nothing ever happened in this county until the murders started, and every old man knew the gossip. Women were dying, and there were no clues. Sheriff Mike had effectively put a lid on the paranormal aspect of the case.

Jeff sat in his car and stared at the door of the jailhouse. He was contemplating his near future. Ida had been right. It was a small town. He could bag groceries at the local market, run a cash register at the only gas station in town, or pick up garbage every weekday morning around the neighborhoods in a garbage truck. The whole point of joining the Marines was to leave this town and his father behind. The shrapnel that had shredded his lower legs meant he could never be an active Marine again. He could walk, he could run, but he could not carry a pack on his back. The Marines had offered him a desk job. Pushing paper on the new recruits as they arrived at boot camp. Jeff couldn't think of a more boring job, so he opted to finish his term of service and come home.

Why home? The world was full of interesting places. Beaches, deserts, and city lights did not appeal to Jeff. He had to face facts. Home was a warm blanket on a cold night. He was comfortable here. People knew his name. Anywhere else in the world, he would be alone. Lying alone in a hospital bed while his legs healed, Jeff had yearned for home.

Jeff opened the car door and got out. Holding his head high, he opened the metal door of the jailhouse, and stepped into a new beginning.

Billy looked up from his desk and said, "Your father is in the back."

Jeff just nodded to Billy, and passed the desks in the office. As usual, Greg was on patrol, so there were two empty desks behind Billy's desk. Billy was pushing seventy years old, so he was more of a secretary than an actual officer. Mike, the Sheriff, did not have the heart to fire a man who had lost his wife to breast cancer. Billy's life rotated around going home and being in the office.

Jeff knocked on the frame of the door to get his father's attention. "Got a moment?"

Mike put down the file he was reading and motioned his son into the office. He sat back in his chair and waited.

Jeff stood in the door frame, and asked, "Is the job still open?"

Mike motioned for Jeff to take a seat in front of his desk, and said, "Let's talk."

Jeff sat in the chair and waited for his father to speak.

Mike contemplated for a moment and then said, "It has been four years since you left to join the Marines. I do not recognize the son who left. You know, I was in Vietnam."

"Yes, but you never talked about it."

"Yeah, well. You don't exactly want to tell your son about the gruesome stories of war. But I think now you would understand. I know you received the Purple Heart for being injured during your duty."

"Yes," replied Jeff.

"Well, someday I may show you the ribbons I received in the war, but right now I see a man sitting in front of me, and no longer the boy. I see the look in your eyes that only men have after they have come close to death. I saw that a lot in the war. I think you are strong enough to handle the pain. At least, that's how I raised you."

Mike reached into a drawer in his desk and grabbed a folder. He slapped it down on the edge of the desk facing Jeff. "Here is the application to become an officer. First, you have to go to Columbia, South Carolina to take a psychological test. Next, you got to pass a physical. You don't think your injury will be a problem?"

"No, I don't believe so."

"Great. The third thing is gun aptitude. You will also have to go to Columbia for that test and certification. Last, but not least, you must pass an exam on the code and conduct as well as basic laws of the state. Also taken in Columbia. After that, I can swear you in as an officer. You know, before your mom died of lung cancer, we talked about your future."

"I didn't know that."

"Yeah, well. She knew you were planning on joining the Marines when you came of age after high school. She wanted that for you, but she made me promise to offer you a job. Don't get me wrong. I think the Marines turned a boy into a man. Just don't fuck it up."

Jeff reached for the file and said, "I won't fuck it up."

"One more thing. Have you talked to Sandra about the murders? I would do it myself, but you know how the town is, she would be pegged as a suspect."

"The only thing she knows is, yes, it is supernatural."

"Well, all the more reason to keep the FBI out of it. I won't have my town on the six o'clock news. Make sure she understands I will not take pity on this monster."

"I believe she understands." Jeff thought, I don't think you would understand. "I will keep you informed if anything comes to light. I am sure Sandra would help if she could."

"Yeah, well, I might not have a choice if there is another murder. The FBI calls me every day for an update, and I think they want a scapegoat. I don't want anybody in my town to get hurt, so keep me informed and in the loop. Got it?"

"Got it." Jeff walked out of the office. He had a feeling being a boyfriend of a witch could interfere with being an officer of the law, but he would not give up Ida.

As Jeff's Nissan pulled out of the parking spot, a malicious creature watched from the alley across the street. Her red hair seemed to vibrate in the golden sunlight of the morning. She had followed Jeff hoping to find the one who took her hand. The stump was wrapped in an old white t-shirt. Puss had worked its way into the makeshift bandage; turning it dirty yellow. The eyes of the thing showed no remorse over losing a hand, but her brain cried for vengeance. The snout in the middle of her head expelled a rush of air and putrid snot. Myra used the stump of her hand to wipe the snot from the slimy forehead. After losing her hand, Myra had become more of a creature than the vestiges of humanity she once had in common with her mother.

Chapter Nineteen

Ida and Sandra had safely made it out of the woods in the middle of the night. Sandra's grandmother's charm worked. Neither talked while winding their way through brush and obstacles in the middle of the night. The dark places in the woods scared them both. At any moment, Ida expected some creature to lunge out of the dark. Sandra was truly scared. She knew what a rabid vampire could do to a human body with its sharp claws and fangs. She had not felt safe until they both flopped down on their bedrolls in the tent at two o'clock in the morning. After basically running through the woods, they both fell asleep in the warm embrace of civilization and warm bedrolls.

Not exactly comfortable on the hard ground, Sandra woke up to the noises of the other campers. She lay on her back for a moment, just enjoying the mountain air and the solitude of the tent. She checked her watch. It was ten o'clock in the morning. Rolling over, she nudged Ida before backing out of the tent. She grabbed a butane stove and started warming coffee on the small burner. She had packed a large thermos of coffee for mornings just like this beautiful day in the woods. The metal thermos inundated the morning air with the sharp aroma of dark coffee. Ida finally crawled out of the tent.

Ida said, "Thank goodness. I totally forgot about coffee. I did pack some cinnamon buns though."

"Sounds like the makings of breakfast."

Both of them sat on the ground and ate a breakfast of sticky cinnamon buns and a little better than lukewarm coffee. Each of them was gathering their thoughts.

"So," said Ida. "What do you know about vampires?"

Sandra wiped the sticky sugar from her finger tips onto her shorts and replied, "A vampire is one of the Night People. Usually, they keep to themselves in the dark parts of the woods. If you ever felt a creepy sensation run down your spine while walking at night in the woods, then you probably had vampires tracking your movements. They usually trap their prey and suckle on the blood before releasing the animal back into the wild. They live in tribes and never bother humans.

You could say they are like the Yeti in the Pacific Northwest. Everyone has seen a Yeti, but nobody can prove there are Yeti. They have enough intelligence to know that people would hunt them down and exterminate them like other Night People. A prime example is the basilisk. It could kill with a glance, and humans feared it. Here in America, they wiped them out early before the Native American people could tell them it was a harmless lizard unless provoked. After that genocide, Night People mostly keep to themselves in the remote places of America. But a rabid vampire is different. It kills. Plain and simple, it kills without remorse. I am surprised the Night People have not slain it, because it is an unthinking creature that could expose the tribe."

"What do they look like?"

Sandra poured herself another cup of coffee, and replied, "I guess you could say they look like monkeys with bat heads. They are completely covered in fur, and about four feet tall with long legs and arms. If you have ever seen a bat head, then you know how it looks. A nose sort of pushed into the face with large fangs and pointed ears. They are strong and fast, but they sleep during the day. That is probably why the fairy will lead us to it during the day."

"How do we kill it? Do we have to stake it in the heart?"

Sandra laughed, "It's true cinema has made some vampires seem glamorous, but the truth is they are just another unique form of a creature created by Mother Earth. We will kill it with this."

Sandra reached into her bag, and pulled out a .38 caliber pistol. An old revolver, dark and heavy, not like the shiny Saturday Night Specials made today.

"This was my great uncle's revolver. Loud, but easy to shoot."

"Well, I really do not know anything about guns, so you hold onto that. So, what do we do for the next couple hours before the fairy shows?"

"I don't know about you, but I think I am going to walk up to the utility building and see if they have a shower. Then maybe another snack before our adventure."

Since most campers woke up at dawn, the facilities were mostly empty. Ida and Sandra found a row of shower heads with no privacy. The building had been partitioned for women on the left side and men on the right. It reminded Ida of the showers in high school. Standing next to each other, the cool shower water washed over their naked bodies. Sandra's sun kissed skin, except for the white triangular silhouette of her bikini bottoms, contrasted with Ida's walnut brown skin. Sandra's breasts were a little bit larger with pink nipples, while Ida's breasts were perter with brown nipples. Both had lean bodies with flat stomachs. Sandra's hips were wider than Ida's slender hips. Coarse blonde hair versus coarse black hair. They could have been twins if twins could be night and day.

After their showers both of them hit up the vending machines. Sugary goodness and soda pop made a fine snack. While they ate, they watched a few kids play basketball in the dirt with a basket high in the air. Not exactly regulation, but the kids seemed to have fun. After their snack, they walked back to the campsite holding hands. Each of them yearned for a little comfort.

At exactly the stroke of noon, Nila the fairy popped like a sound of a bubble bursting in front of Sandra's face and said, "Meet me east, past the waterfall." She disappeared just as suddenly as she had appeared.

Sandra hid the gun in her cargo shorts pocket. Without saying a word, they trekked to the waterfall. Glancing at the sun, Sandra set a course east of the waterfall. After a couple of minutes, Nila flew out of a small fern growing on the forest floor. She did not say a word, but led them through the forest. The fairy could fly over any obstacle, but she stuck to the natural animal trails for the humans. After an hour of flying, Nila stopped in midair and beckoned Sandra forward.

She whispered, "Over that hill is a tree deadfall. The vampire has built a nest to roost under the tree. You will have to go inside to see the vampire. Be warned, I believe it is awake. If you succeed, I will be waiting here for our bargain."

Sandra turned to Ida and said, "Listen. You don't have go in with me, Ida. I have the gun."

Ida replied, "Yeah, well, I have a stick." She picked up a large branch off the forest floor, and bent it to see if it broke. She motioned with her eyes for Sandra to continue.

Sandra, followed by Ida, crept over the small hill. At its summit, the girls could see the deadfall tree. Large sticks and branches had formed a sort of cave out of trees, making a home for the vampire.

Ida whispered, "Do we have a plan?"

Sandra replied, "I thought I was going to be able to see, but that tunnel looks dark. Walking into a dark cave is not my idea of fun."

"Do you think I could spook it? I can go to the side, and bang on the tree with the stick."

"That might work. I can only see one way in or out so let's try that."

Sandra crept down the hill towards the entrance, while Ida flanked her on the left. Sandra felt she had a good view of the entrance, so she stopped and waved Ida on towards the dead tree. Ida pushed her way through some blueberry bushes to the left of the makeshift cave. She leaned against the dead tree next to the cave and nodded to Sandra while raising the stick. She beat the stick three times against the fallen tree.

The side of the cave nearest Ida exploded, sending dead branches directly at Ida's face. With its long claws, the vampire took a swipe at Ida's shoulder. The shirt and flesh parted easily. Blood ran down Ida's front and side. Without thinking, Ida dropped down onto her stomach. Two shots rang out. One shot struck the vampire in the belly. The other shot clipped an ear. Screaming, the vampire flung itself towards Sandra. Lining up the shot, Sandra squeezed the trigger. The third shot pierced the heart. The vampire struck the ground, and it was dead.

Sandra ran to Ida. Kneeling down, she asked, "Are you alright?"

Ida rolled her shoulder up to look at and said, "I think so. I may need some stitches, but I think I'm alright."

"I knew the shot was dangerous but when you dropped like that it gave me a clear shot." Sandra untied the decorative knotted bandana around her neck. She pressed it against the gash on Ida's shoulder.

"Believe me, I am glad you took the shot. I have never seen something move that fast. Help me up."

Sandra stood Ida up on her feet. They walked over to the dead vampire. Shoving it with her foot, Sandra confirmed that it was dead.

"What now?" asked Ida, holding the bandana on her wound.

"I don't know."

Nila appeared out of the thin air and replied, "The vampire tribe will eat him."

Ida answered, "That's kind of disgusting."

Nila said, "Maybe, but they cannot leave a trace of their existence. If your people discovered the body, it would put the Night People as well as the Faye in jeopardy."

"Does this mean you are not going to help us?" asked Ida.

"Yes, we will keep our bargain. The monster you describe sounds manipulated by something even more evil. Do you know the Home Maker blessing for Pahit Lidah?"

"Yes," answered Ida. "But that spell is for abusive men."

"Yes. But when you add the tear drops of the Faye, the ward will keep all things out." Nila hovered over Sandra's hand. She then dropped a tiny leather flagon into Sandra's palm. "One drop per spool." Nila vanished.

Sandra asked, "Do you know what she was talking about?"

"Yes. Pahit Lidah is an East Indian goddess. We'll do it later. Right now, my shoulder hurts."

They followed the animal trails back to the campsite. Immediately, a helpful camper used a pay phone located at the utility building to call the Forest Service. A medic drove into camp thirty minutes later. Ida explained to the Forest Service medic that she had fallen off some rocks and hurt herself. With deft hands, the medic cleaned the wound and stitched the three gashes closed. Six stitches later, the medic explained to Ida that the stitches needed to come out in a couple of weeks. She could do it herself, or go to a local clinic to have the stitches removed. Ida thanked the man and promised to go to the clinic.

Chapter Twenty

Sandra pushed the Bug down the road doing slightly over the speed limit. She wanted to be back to Clear View by dark. Normally, the trip lasted for about two and a half hours. With no stops, and skirting the speed limits in towns and on highways, she figured on shaving off thirty minutes. Something was driving her; a gut feeling. The near-death experience of killing the vampire had added an urgency to keep her coven safe. She hoped the ward would end the conflict with the Blood Witch and the Grendel. After being thwarted, it was possible they would move on. While driving, she did consider taking a more offensive approach to combating the monsters, but the duo set of ilk were powerful and she could lose her life as well as anyone helping her. Almost losing Ida to the vampire weighed heavily on her soul.

Ida slept in the passenger seat. The seat was leaned back and Ida was curled up into a little ball. The medic had given her a course of antibiotics to take as well as some tablets of five hundred milligram ibuprofen. Staying awake had been uncomfortable at best, so she had decided to sleep and let her body heal.

The Bug pulled into the alley behind Sandra's shop; the gas dial almost touching the empty line. Two hours of sunlight were left before dark, they had made the trip in under two hours.

Sandra said, "We're home."

Ida rolled onto her back and rubbed the sleep from her eyes like a child. She winced when she moved her shoulder. "What time is it?" She asked.

"A couple of hours before dark. Does the ward spell need to be in the light or the dark?"

Ida pulled up the seat to a sitting position and answered, "It is best in the light. I need a stone altar, four orange candles, and five spools of thread."

"I have a flat granite bolder in my garden, and I can retrieve the other items. Have a seat in my lounge chair in the backyard to rest."

Sandra exited the car and opened a gate in the back of the fence. Ida lost sight of her. Ida took stock of her situation. She tested her shoulder. The pain was moderate, but she could use it.

Sandra came out of the back door carrying the items. She looked at Ida in the lounge chair and asked, "Are you up to this?"

"Yeah, I feel better than I look. The spell is pretty simple. The goddess Pahit Lidah turned abusive men to stone. To stay safe, East Indian women prayed to the goddess over spools of thread asking for protection. After the goddess blessed the spools of thread, the women would cut a line of thread and place the thread on the threshold of every entrance to their home. The ward would turn away any man who would harm a woman. The ward would play tricks on the man's mind and they would basically forget why they came, and just turn around and leave. As for the fairy tears, I do not know how it will add to the equation."

"What do you need from me?"

"I've got it." She held out her hand for the instruments needed for the spell.

Ida sat in front of the flat boulder in the corner of the garden. She placed four candles in a square, and the spools of thread in the middle. She lit the candles with a match. Watching the flames flicker, she concentrated on her chakra. She could feel the energy of the flames and the heavy earth of the stone. She needed to be the bridge between the stone, the flame, and the spools of thread.

Repeating a litany, she invoked the spell, "Blessed be the Goddess Pahit Lidah."

While she repeated the words, she concentrated on her chakra. The chakra lines in her body tingled. The flames of the candles turned from yellow and red to a bright blue. The blue flames enveloped the spools of thread. Without losing a beat of the invocation, Ida poured the tears of the fairies onto the spools of thread. The blue flames receded to the candles. The candles' flames turned back to red and yellow.

Ida intoned, "Thank you Goddess Pahit Lidah."

Ida lay flat on the grass for a moment. The pain in her shoulder had eased to a small throb. She took a breath and said, "That's it."

"How do you feel?" asked Sandra.

"Actually, pretty good."

"So, what now?" asked Sandra.

"What do you mean? We use the thread."

"I know that will be a deterrent for the monster, but I think we may need to go on the offensive."

"Maybe finding out why the Blood Witch has a vendetta?" asked Ida.

"Yeah, maybe that could help. I just have a feeling this will end in bloodshed."

"Blood has already been spilled. Our sisters and brother lie in the grave," said Ida with conviction.

Sighing, Sandra replied, "I just don't want anyone else to get hurt."

Later that day, the sun was setting on the downtown of Clear View. For the past two hours, Sandra had handed out the spools of thread to the coven. The coven agreed to stay in pairs. Each of them voiced an opinion about what should be done. They were scared, and tired of being locked up in their homes. Sandra convinced them that the pair of monsters would move on. It would just take time and patience.

At full dark, the street lights came on; lighting the sidewalks and downtown stores. The pillars of light were spaced evenly on the sidewalks of the downtown area. A bar at the far end of the street pumped music into the air. People were gathering on another hot summer's night.

Sandra's doors were normally locked tight with the shades pulled down by this time of night, but she had been talking to the members of her coven in the middle of the store. Now, she was tired and ready for bed. Already, Ida slept in her queen-sized bed upstairs. Sandra thought about joining her and turning in early. She approached the glass door of her shop to pull down the shade and lock the door.

Myra stood outside the glass door. She wore a ragged, green summer dress. The hem was torn and Myra was barefoot. The stump of her hand was wrapped in a clean dressing made of yellow strips of cloth. In her other hand, she held a bowie knife. The blade was eight inches long and two inches wide with a serrated edge riding on top of the blade. The handle was made of elk bone and the steel tang pressed into Myra's palm.

"Closing early?" asked Myra.

Sandra opened the door and stood at arm's length back from the threshold. "Just waiting on you. I would invite you in but that could be the end for me. Before you come in, could you tell me why you and your mother are targeting my people?"

"Put simply, I wanted to feed on human flesh. My mother suggested your coven. She has a bone to pick with you personally, but only your grandmother knows all the facts."

"The witch my grandmother banned from the coven."

"Precisely. My mother wanted you to be last, but things have changed." She held up her bandaged stump. "After I kill you, I am going upstairs to kill the bitch who took my hand."

Myra held the knife out in front and stepped forward. The nostril on its forehead trembled. Myra stopped and said, "I smell magic."

Myra's face turned ugly. The frown on her lips was nothing compared to the malice in Myra's eyes. Myra probed the entrance to the shop with the tip of the blade. The tip turned to stone. Myra dropped it before the transformation of the steel to stone reached the guard. The knife clattered on the step of the shop. The knife was barely discernable as the color of the sidewalk concrete matched the steel knife transformed to stone.

"Are you sure you don't want to come in?" asked Sandra.

"Now you've done it. You made momma mad." Myra walked across the street to the blue Buick.

Sandra had no idea what Myra meant by that comment, but she was happy the ward worked.

Chapter Twenty-One

As Vivian drove the car down dark streets, Myra slammed the dashboard with her good hand. Myra acted like a petulant child of three or a hormonal sixteen-year-old girl. Myra oscillated between angry outbursts and intense crying spells. After ten minutes of tumultuous anger, she settled down to sniffles and occasional sobs.

Vivian asked, "Do you want to talk?"

Myra replied, "NO."

Myra sat in the passenger seat. The wheels in her brain turned at a fabulous clip. She wanted to kill and maim the witches, especially the one who took her hand. She fantasized about killing Sandra; cutting her with the knife until only a bloody corpse remained and snacking on the bits of carved out flesh. Myra wanted to leave Ida lame. She envisioned cutting off Ida's hands, scooping out her eyeballs with her fingernails, and leaving her to live a miserable life. She sobbed again, because she had been robbed of her vengeance. The ward was too powerful. She could stalk them outside of their homes, but the dangers of being caught outweighed the pleasure of killing them. The wheels in her mind continued to turn. She wanted an answer for the dilemma. She wanted a gruesome death for both of the Nature Witches. She had an epiphany.

"Mother?" asked Myra. "Could you summon a demon?"

Vivian shook her head and said, "It is too dangerous."

"But mother, they took my hand," pleaded Myra.

"It could kill me," said Vivian quietly.

Myra screamed, "I don't care!" Myra sobbed and said, "Please mother, kill the bitch."

Vivian paused for a moment and said, "The spell would need a lot of blood."

Excited, Myra replied, "I will give you all the blood you need."

"No child," said Vivian. She thought for a moment and said, "Remember the spell in '72?"

"The spell to enthrall a man?"

"Yes."

Myra squirmed in her seat and said, "I don't like the smell."

"Well, homeless drug addicts are not known for bathing."

"Fine, and where will we find a homeless person in this town?"

"We won't, but we will find one in Columbia. Kidnapping a homeless person is the easy part. Not getting caught is the hard part."

"I won't allow us to get caught," said Myra. "I can break their necks while they sleep."

"For this much blood, they have to be kept alive. We will have to exsanguinate the body right before the spell. It has to be hot blood."

"Can we do it tomorrow?" pleaded Myra.

"Myra, this is going to be dangerous. For both of us. If I can't subjugate the demon, it will kill us both."

"Ok," said Myra. "But when?"

"First, we must gather other components for the spell, and the spell has to be performed during a full moon. We have two weeks to prepare."

"Then those bitches won't know what hit them," laughed Myra.

Chapter Twenty-Two

During the light of the day, Sandra's displays in the window of her shop almost glowed. The small silver chains set with rubies, emeralds, and sapphires cast a kaleidoscope of colors on the glass panes of her storefront windows. If you did not know any better, the necklaces were just pretty objects, but some of the stones were infused with simple charms. Some for luck; emeralds, some for health; sapphires, some for mental health; rubies. Most importantly, all the charms were created to help bring joy into the wearers' lives. One of the creeds for a Nature Witch was to bring harmony to life.

As usual, Sandra sat behind the counter of the shop. Usually, she liked to flip through the latest magazine, but today she perused a large leather-bound tome. Freshly painted pink fingernails tapped the counters surface as she tried to read the Latin text. The tome was an amalgamation of spells and some history of magic. She had purchased it years ago in a bookstore in Columbia. More of a footnote in her collection of books, now she hoped it would shine a light on her current situation by telling her how to kill a Blood Witch. It was a slow process. She knew how to read Latin, but it had been years since she had put her mind to the test.

The cow bell clanged as Jeff walked into the store and said, "Not exactly easy reading."

Jeff wore blue jeans and a green t-shirt embossed with the latest logo of a shoe company. The shirt pulled against the muscles of his chest and the sleeves were tight on his biceps. Sandra could see why Ida was attracted to the young man physically. As for her, he was still just a kid looking for trouble.

"Sorry Jeff, Ida is resting upstairs at the moment," said Sandra.

With a little bit of panic in his voice, he asked, "Is she OK?"

Sandra closed the tome and replied, "She's fine. We had a little run in with a vampire a couple of days ago. Her arm required a few stitches."

"A vampire. You're joking, right?"

"A little bit of advice, dating a witch brings more baggage than usual. Besides, yes, she needed stitches to close the wound, but she is fine."

"Baggage huh," said Jeff. Jeff did not feel comfortable talking about Ida's and his relationship so he changed the subject. "Ida asked me to run a plate for her."

"And?"

"Well, it's a little weird. The plate came back with Vivian McDonnel, but the license said she was a hundred and ten years old."

"Well, that explains a lot."

"How so?"

"Vivian has around ten years to live; assuming she was in her twenties when she had sex with the satyr. The spell to keep her eternal youth granted by the satyr will expire after exactly one hundred years."

"How do you know this?"

"I consulted a Grey Witch and she told me about the satyr spell. There are not too many spells a witch can cast to keep a youthful appearance. Sure, you can use glamour spells to appear young, but to be truly young, only a satyr can grant that."

"Well, she also has a rap sheet three pages long. Mostly petty theft, some prostitution, but for some time now she has turned her talents to being a con artist. Several family members of old people claimed she drained their mother or father dry. Charges were brought, but the old people backed her."

"A Blood Witch can talk to spirits. The old people must have paid her to talk to lost relatives. To do the spell, though, the old people must have given up their own blood. You don't exactly want to tell your children that part, so it makes sense they would back her."

"What are you going to do about these two?"

"The less you know, the better."

"Well, like you said, dating a witch brings baggage."

Sandra stopped for a moment, but she made up her mind about Jeff. He could also be in danger and being ignorant could cost him his life.

"Well, at the moment, we have protection in our homes now. The monster cannot cross the threshold of our homes. Most of the coven thinks they will move on, but the monster lost a hand, and the Blood Witch wants revenge."

"How did it lose a hand?"

"Ida stabbed it in the hand with that knife we cursed."

Jeff shuffled his feet. He did not want to think about that night. That night, magic became real for him and it was not pretty.

Sandra said, "Also, I am trying to find a spell to kill the Blood Witch. It has been difficult. Nature Witches are not exactly aggressive hunters like Blood Witches, but I am hopeful I can find something before the next attack."

"You don't think she's done?"

"No, I do not."

"Why not just shoot the bitch?"

"It's not exactly that easy to kill a witch. Especially one with eternal youth for a hundred years. She heals fast, and the monster will not be easy to defeat as well."

"Well, if you need anything, let me know. I am going to be out of town for a week. I'm going to Columbia to take some tests to become a Sheriff's Officer."

"Really?"

"I know. It's not a glamourous job, but it's better than bagging groceries."

"Actually, I think it will be a good fit. No matter what trouble you looked for there was always a boy scout hiding in the weeds."

"You think it's a good fit?"

"I have known you for years, and yes, I think you will do well."

"Ok. Just tell Ida I will be gone for a week. I don't know exactly where I'll be staying, so can I call her here?"

"Absolutely."

Sandra watched him go. She really did believe in him. He had always been a wild child, but with a good heart. His criminal shenanigans were mostly harmless. She believed Jeff had just been trying to be rebellious against his father.

Sandra turned back to the book. The revelation that the Blood Witch was almost immortal for a hundred years would make finding a spell to stop her more difficult, but now she had something to work with to stop her. If she could reverse the process, then ninety years of hard living could catch up to her in one moment.

Sandra flipped the pages of the book. The tome was more a reference guide than an actual spell book. Hopefully, it would yield a glimmer of hope. Faye magic was nefarious, but not unstoppable.

The sun high in the sky brought the heat of another summer day. The Blood Witch gathered the elements for her spell. The Nature Witch continued her research. Who would be the first to succeed?

Chapter Twenty-Three

The motel room looked like a Nineteen Seventy's party would start at any moment. The room had seen pills piled on the nightstand, and cocaine forming lines on the dresser. The old motel had history but now it was just a cheap motel in downtown Columbia. The couple running the motel could not afford renovations, so the rooms could almost be considered nostalgic. The bedroom furniture was all sand-colored wood. The small dining room table stuck in a corner had a Formica yellow top. The gold shag carpet had seen better days. The couple who owned the motel had turned it around. No longer used for parties, the motel was family friendly and clean. Besides, Jeff could not afford a five-star hotel and he felt comfortable and safe in the worn-out motel.

Jeff lounged on the bed, propped up by pillows. The week of hell was done. The grueling tests of both physical and mental rigor had sapped Jeff's strength and patience. A certain amount of mental anguish had accompanied the tests. They never told him if he passed the tests. After each ordeal, they just shook his hand and told him where to be the next day. He was told the results took time to compile and he would receive the grades next week. Jeff believed they just wanted to see him sweat, that they were gauging his reaction to the abuse.

City noise filtered through the window. The streets were crowded with people going to the local bars in downtown Columbia at night. The noise annoyed Jeff. He looked at the clock on the stand. It was a quarter till ten. The sun had set, and the revelry had begun.

He considered calling Ida. He had not spoken to her all week. He missed her. He wanted to hear her laugh. He thought, fuck it and picked up the phone receiver cradled on this block of plastic called a phone. He dialed nine to get a line out.

"Hello?" asked Ida.

"It's not too late, is it?"

"Oh Jeff, no it is not too late. I just now started to wind down. How did the tests go?"

"OK, I guess. They won't tell me the results until next week. I think the only trouble I had was the physical. I had to carry a dummy on my shoulder up a flight of stairs, and it was slow going with my injured legs. I don't know why they asked me to do that. I mean, it's not like I'm going to be a fire fighter."

"I wouldn't worry about it. I'm sure you did just fine. It's Friday night, why aren't you hitting the clubs?"

Jeff laughed and said, "The last thing I want to do is deal with hot heads and women shaking their little butts. The college boys can smell an old hick like me."

"You're not a hick. Besides, most of those boys know momma's house and the dorm room. When I was in college, most of the boys only had two things in mind, sex and booze."

"I do miss sex."

"I miss you too."

"Well, anyway, tell me something about your college days. Did I really miss something?"

Ida laughed and said, "God no. Most of the boys didn't have a clue when it came to sex. And most of the girls only thought they knew what sex was."

"So, you had sex with girls?"

"I dabbled. Does that offend you?"

"No. Not at all. In fact, it kind of turns me on."

"Well, most of the boys in college couldn't wrap their minds around it. You would think they would be more open, but prejudices are everywhere. Ok, my turn. Who was the first girl you kissed?"

"Oh boy. That seems like a long time ago." Jeff thought for a moment and replied, "Her name was Laura. I was twelve and she was fourteen."

"Oh, you like the older ladies. Did she teach you anything?"

"As a matter of fact, she taught me how to French kiss."

"Well, she did a good job."

"My turn. Who was your first boyfriend?"

Ida laughed and said, "Believe it or not, I was eight years old. Todd liked taking me to the movies. He was eight years old too. We never did more than hold hands. Funny thing, he ended up being a car thief, but he was so sweet when he was young."

"Car thief huh. You liked bad boys from the get go."

"Well, I like you don't I"

"I did date this bad girl in high school. She was a rocker chick with jeans and big hair. She smoked cigarettes and had a foul mouth. It didn't last long. She told me I was boring."

"I thought you were a hellion back in the day. At least, that's Sandra's story."

"I guess I wasn't bad enough. She ended up marrying a biker and had three kids. Last time I saw her, she looked pretty rough."

"Barely made it out alive."

Jeff laughed and said, "Just barely. How old were you when you lost your virginity?"

"How old were you?"

"Like I said, bad girl. She broke my cherry in sophomore year."

"Well, I lost my virginity in ninth grade. Believe it or not, the boy was from middle school eighth grade, but God, he was beautiful. Long blonde hair and he was taller than me. I can't think of a single boy more beautiful than him. It was over before it seemed we begun. We only dated for a couple of months and then the school year ended and he moved away."

"Do you ever think about him?"

"Sometimes. It's easy to think he was perfect because the relationship was so short. He took me to a dance at the middle school. It was the first time I felt pretty."

"I'll have to thank him for that."

Ida hesitated and asked, "Here's the big one. Who was the first girl you were in love with?"

"That's easy, the first girl I kissed."

Ida laughed and said, "No. Really?"

"I know it sounds corny, but we dated for the entire summer. We went to the movies. We swam in an inground pool in her back yard all day. We would sit for hours and talk about what we wanted in life. Superficial stuff; we wanted to be popular at school, things like that. I can't think of a better summer in my life. Some of it was physical, but she taught me so much about life in general. She broke my heart at the end of the summer. She was going to high school, and couldn't be dating a younger boy. I don't know if she loved me, but I fell head over heels for her."

"Oh, you had a huge crush. Do you know what happened to her?"

"Later that year, her parents divorced and she moved away. I don't know what happened to her. What about you. Who was your first love?"

"I don't know about love. I don't know if I have ever loved someone more than you."

"Are you crying?"

"Just a little bit."

"I don't want to sound dramatic. I am not saying I love you because you said it first, but I do love you."

"Thank you. I have a lot to process. When are you coming home?"

"I'll be there tomorrow."

"Can I see you?"

"Are you kidding? You'll be my first stop in town."

"Great. I'll see you tomorrow. Goodnight."

"Goodnight, girl of my dreams." Jeff hung up the phone.

He stared at the phone for a moment. For the first time in a long time, he felt at peace.

Chapter Twenty-Four

Jeff drove his car on the downtown streets of Clear View. He marveled at the difference between the quaint small town and the big city of Columbia. Downtown Clear View adhered to the American dream. Small shops, bars, restaurants, and a small theater lined the main drag of the center of town. The street seemed bright and cheery with artisan lamp posts dotting the white cement sidewalks. Intermittently, small trees full of bright green leaves adorned the sidewalk. Some stores had plant boxes attached to storefronts with a cadre of flowers. People strode down the street seeming to have no particular destination in mind. In contrast, Columbia streets were littered with trash. The haphazard store fronts in Columbia had small windows, or large windows with rebar protecting the stores from theft. Aligning the street, tall metal posts with yellow lamps threw yellow light onto the surface of the grey concrete sidewalk. Jeff thought, "You can have the city." He was proud to be a small-town boy.

Jeff parked his car in a spot outside of Ida's apartment building. His nerves jangled. In the pit of his stomach, a small knot seemed to have developed. In one moment, he wanted to run up the stairs and pound on the door, and a second later he wondered if baring his feelings over the phone had been a good idea. What if she laughed at him? What if it had been a hoax? He could not remember a time in his life that he had felt so vulnerable as this moment.

Jeff methodically plodded up the stairs to Ida's apartment. He hesitated for one moment before knocking on the door. Ida swung the door open and all Jeff could do was smile at the most beautiful woman he had ever known. Ida did not hesitate. She jerked him forward and planted a kiss firmly on his mouth. She pulled him into the apartment and shimmied out of her night gown, then pulled Jeff's t-shirt over his head. Wearing only a pair of panties, Ida unbuckled Jeff's belt. Forcing her hand down the front of Jeff's parachute pants, she reached for the back of his head to firmly plant a kiss on his lips. Jeff undid his pants and almost headbutted her as he kneeled down to rip the black pants off, but they stuck to his hips. He tried to pull them over his hips but the pants would not budge.

Jeff said, "I have a problem."

Ida laughed, "What are those anyway?"

Jeff looked down. He wore a pair of parachute pants made of polyester. Several silver metal zippers were sewn into the legs. He said sheepishly, "I got them in Columbia."

"Hold on," said Ida. She pulled the pants back up. She said, "Girls have this problem all the time."

"Really?"

"Just trust me. Lay down on your back, and raise your hips." Ida nabbed the pant cuffs at the bottom and slipped the pants right off Jeff's body. "Well, that is definitely not a girl."

Twenty minutes later, both of them lay naked on the living room floor with their clothes strewn haphazardly about them. Ida's head rested on Jeff's outstretched arm. Even though the apartment had air conditioning, both of them were drenched in sweat.

"I don't want to ruin the moment," said Jeff. "But you are taking precautions?"

Ida smiled and twisted her head to look at Jeff. Her hair was matted on one side of her face. She dreaded running a comb through the tassels of her hair, but she loved that Jeff tugged her hair during sex. She answered, "Yes. I am a contemporary woman. Would you like a glass of sweet tea?"

"Oh, God yes," exclaimed Jeff.

Ida rolled off Jeff's arm, and sashayed to the kitchen. As she walked, she asked, "You are checking out my ass?"

"Absolutely!"

Ida brought two glasses of tea. She motioned for Jeff to join her on the couch. After downing half the glass, Ida placed a hand on Jeff's knee, and asked, "So, when can you bring the handcuffs?"

After Jeff chugged the tea he replied, "I hope I will know this coming Monday."

"Are you excited?"

"Honestly, I didn't think I would be, but I believe I am."

"A copper, a flat foot, a man in blue. I have never dated an officer of the law. Are you going to arrest me for breaking sexual statutes from archaic state laws?"

"I would have to arrest myself."

Ida snuggled herself next to Jeff. He put his arm around her shoulders. She asked, "Quick question? Who gets the shower first?"

"I think I will have another glass of tea while you take a shower."

Ida slapped his taut belly and headed for the shower. Jeff stood up and headed for the refrigerator. He reached for the pitcher in the fridge and saw a half of an apple pie in a tinfoil pie tray. He figured Ida would not mind if he had a piece. As he cut out a slice he wondered why he had been so nervous earlier. She obviously loved him. Sometimes an act spoke a thousand words.

Jeff polished off the last morsel of the pie when Ida stepped out of the bathroom. A towel wrapped around her waist; her lovely breasts were flush from the hot water.

Ida said, "I see you found something to eat. I'm hungry and I want to go somewhere for brunch."

"I could eat. By the way, why are you not at Sandra's apartment? Is the beast dead?"

"No. But the ward we have around our homes makes it impossible for it to enter. You just missed Sandra. We are taking turns staying at our places."

"Where does she sleep?"

"In the bed, silly."

A small frown creased Jeff's brow.

"Oh, no. Don't look at me like that. I explained my feelings to you about the coven."

Jeff smiled and slouched in the chair. He said, "I guess I will need time to reconcile our relationship with your relationship to the coven."

Ida walked up to him and placed a kiss on top of his head. "There is nothing to reconcile. You are mine."

Jeff grabbed her and dropped her into his lap. He kissed her full on the mouth and then said, "And you are mine. By the way, how does one become a witch?"

"It's simpler than you think and not entirely up to you. What makes me different than the average person is I can channel energy. It is something you are born with. Some people can devote their whole lives to learning about witch craft and never be able to perform magic."

Ida slapped him on the shoulder and said, "Get in the shower. Get dressed. Then you are taking me to brunch."

Jeff untangled himself from Ida and said, "Yes, ma'am."

Ida smiled as she checked out Jeff's tiny butt. She could not think of anyone else in her life that made her feel a radiation of love like Jeff. It scared her a little. She unfocused her eyes just for a moment to read Jeff's aura. He glowed bright blue. At the moment, the aura emanating from him meant he was perfectly content. She hugged herself for one moment to make her feelings real.

Chapter Twenty-Five

Vivian whistled a little ditty as she worked on the molds for the ritual candles. She sat cross-legged in the middle of the floor. In her hand she held a flimsy, cardboard plate. With a dollop of glue in the center of the plate, she held a long string attached to the plate with the glue. Waiting for the glue to dry, she whistled the song Camp Town Races. On the floor next to her, the first mold was already completed. A simple thing, the mold sported four parts. The plate supported the bottom of the mold and a cardboard toilet paper roll placed in the center of the plate was held in place by tape at the bottom. A string tunneled to the top was held in place with a popsicle stick resting on top of the roll. The toilet roll held the ingredients of the candle in place, while the string naturally permeated the center of the finished candle. The first completed mold just sat there and waited to be filled with pig lard.

She sat waiting for the glue to be tacky so she could construct the second mold. She glanced outside the open door at the twilight. She had sent Myra to a farm three miles through the woods to steal a pig. She had expected Myra to be back by now. Of course, dragging a dead pig through the woods with one hand would be difficult, and Vivian could imagine Myra cursing the brambles, ditches, and other obstacles as she dragged the pig.

Myra stepped into the door frame and said, "It's here."

Vivian replied, "I just need a couple more minutes to finish the second mold. Any problems?"

"I killed the farmer."

"Why, pray child, did you have to kill the farmer? I told you to be discrete."

Myra plopped down onto her bedroll and said, "The damn pig was too loud. It kept squealing as I dragged it through the field. You told me not to kill it in the pen, so the farmer would think it ran away. Well, the farmer came out with a shot gun to stop me. I played the innocent little girl to lure him closer and hit him with the pig."

"Ha, ha, ha. Death by pig. Of all the ways to kill a farmer, that seems almost poetic. What did you do with the body?"

"Well, after wrestling with the pig and the walk through the woods, I was a little hungry. So, I ate his liver and then buried him in the pig pen. I tried to bring the shot gun, but it kept catching onto branches of trees while sticking out of my waistband, so I left it in the woods. I can go get it if you like."

"You can get it later. Take a sharp knife and peel the skin off the back of the pig. Underneath is a layer of fat. Cut that fat out and bring it to me."

Myra went to work on the pig while Vivian finished the mold.

Ten minutes later, Myra brought in the pig fat. Vivian built up the fire in the pot belly stove. The stove had two functions; to keep the room warm in the winter, and as a cook top. Not exactly a modern appliance, the cook top's heat fluctuated from the fire in the belly of the stove. Vivian figured she could work with the stove.

Vivian placed a large skillet on the stove to bring up the temperature of the iron skillet. Working on a small table next to the stove, she cut the pig fat into small one-inch squares. She dropped one piece into the skillet to test the heat. It started frying, so she dumped the rest of the fat into the skillet with a half cup of water. Stirring occasionally, she rendered the pig fat. The trick was keeping the heat in the skillet from burning the grease pouring out of the chunks of pig fat. After all the pieces of fat were a nice golden color, she poured the grease and pig fat into a strainer over a plastic bowl. Shaking the strainer, she separated the chunks from the searing lard. She dumped the chunks back into the skillet, and dumped a bag of once frozen vegetables into the skillet.

Myra asked, "What are the vegetables for?"

Vivian replied, "It's my dinner. Besides, the lard has to cool for a couple of minutes before I pour in your blood."

"My blood. Why my blood?"

Vivian stirred the mixture and said, "I need the blood of a Faye creature for the spell in the candles. Since you are a bastard Faye, it will work."

After she finished cooking her dinner, Vivian gestured Myra forward. Grabbing Myra's hand, she cut the palm with a small knife. Blood dripped into the lard in the bowl. She let go of Myra's hand and stirred the cooling lard. The lard's color turned into a deep red. Dipping her fingertip into the lard, she tested the temperature of the mixture. It was cool enough. She poured the lard into the molds. It would take twenty-four hours to harden in the mold. After the lard hardened, she would cut the toilet paper roll from the candle. Unlike beeswax, the lard candles would be smoky, which she needed for part of the ritual to summon a demon. Also, the candles had to be made out of flesh for the ritual, so she couldn't use beeswax.

Myra asked, "So, is that it?"

Vivian answered, "No. This is a complicated spell to summon a demon. The next thing we need is a piece of vellum."

"What is vellum?"

"It is what they used to write on instead of paper, and it is expensive."

"But we don't have any money."

Irritated, Vivian replied, "I know that. We are going to trade for it. I know a serial rapist in Columbia who owns a bookstore. He likes my concoction because after dosing a woman with it, she does not remember anything for the entire day. She can physically feel that she had been raped, but she has total amnesia for the last twenty-four hours."

Myra laughed and said, "That's rich."

Vivian grinned, and said, "It's a little bit evil."

Neither one cared less about the unfortunate soul that would be violated. For them, it was a game.

Vivian said, "I need you to gather the ingredients for the potion. I need a button mushroom, sassafras root, and a live black widow spider."

Myra replied, "I don't remember this potion."

"You wouldn't. Remember when you wanted to go to Community College? It cost a great deal of money for books, tuition, and that little one-bedroom apartment. Well, I had to make a lot of potions for that bastard. He kept me on the hook for six months until you decided to drop out of college."

"Nobody liked me."

"Of course, they didn't, you were eighty years old even though you looked eighteen, and you hated the homework."

"I didn't hate all of it. Just Dunhill's class. History is so boring and she kept picking on me because I didn't read the assignments every night. She was the first person I thought about eating."

"Well, I think after we kill everyone, we need a lot of seed money to start a new life. I have always wanted to see the west coast."

Myra jumped up and down clapping her hands, "Kill, kill, kill."

"Alright. Go get me the ingredients out of the woods. We have a potion to make."

Chapter Twenty-Six

Jeff found himself sitting in his car again outside the police station. He really wanted to impress Ida. He really liked her. He had been in several serious relationships during his life, but Ida was different. He loved her. Before her, relationships had been fun, but he could not recall actually being in love with any of the girls. He broke girls' hearts. Not intentionally, only because he was not in love with them. He felt very vulnerable at the moment. Talking to his father was the last thing he wanted to do at this moment. The old man had a way of smelling perceived weakness. He could not a make an impression on Ida if he did not get out of the car and see if he got the job. He opened the car door to go inside the police station.

As usual, Billy sat at the desk facing the door. On the phone, Billy ignored Jeff and just pointed with his thumb for Jeff to go to the back office. Jeff walked between the row of desks to the back office where his father had sat supreme for the past thirty years. Jeff walked into the office. His father grinned at him.

"Well, you made it," said Mike the sheriff.

"So, does that mean I got the job?" asked Jeff.

"Yeah, but just barely. You almost didn't pass the physical. After discussing your legs with a doctor, they decided to pass you."

Jeff sat down in a chair, "What about the rest of the tests?"

"They were impressed. Your knowledge of the law and handling a firearm really cemented the job. I was worried your hippy ways would be detrimental to the psychological evaluation, but you did well in that as well."

Jeff laughed and said, "Maybe they are just looking for some modern ways."

"If modern ways are sleeping on people's couches instead of having a place to live, then they can keep it."

"Will you let that go?"

"No, I won't. I can't have my deputies couch surfing, so I am giving you an advance on your paycheck. Here is five hundred dollars."

Mike passed Jeff an envelope filled with twenty-dollar bills. "It's an advance. Not a handout."

"Got it. Speaking of money, what is the salary for sheriff's deputies these days?"

"It comes with a salary of twelve thousand dollars, but, and I mean but, you have to be on-call twenty-four hours a day some weeks. So no drugs or drinking during on call hours. We rotate the on-call weeks between us. Got it?"

"I got it."

"So, what did you think about the evaluations?"

"Not as bad as I thought. I did get to play with The Pig. Why a police force needs that is beyond me."

"A Pig?"

"In the Marines, we called a M60 machine gun The Pig."

"It's probably just something to impress people with. Speaking of impressions, are you still dating that girl?"

"Yes, and you are going to see a lot of her."

Mike grunted and said, "Well, I need you to go back to Columbia for the next two weeks for training. You will learn proper codes for the radio, and state, federal, and local ordinances. If you past the exam at the end, then you're my deputy."

"What do I do with the money if I don't pass?"

"Smart ass. I'll see you in few days. Stop at the desk and give Billy your measurements for the uniform. He'll call it in, so we will have it in a couple days. Also, your sidearm will be a .38 caliber special pistol issued by this office."

"I prefer my 9mm Beretta."

"I know, but this is a small town. We don't need that kind of fire power. Everyone carries a .38, so you will too."

"Anything else?"

"Not at the moment. I will see you in a few days." Mike rubbed the top of his head and said, "Listen. I am proud of you. I have always wanted you to follow in my footsteps. When you went to the Marines, I didn't know if you were coming back. Ok. That's it."

Jeff stood up and exited the office. Jeff felt that compliment. Mike rarely praised him. Jeff felt like he was doing the right thing.

Chapter Twenty-Seven

Vivian drove down the streets of the downtown area of Columbia. She decided earlier to leave Myra at the shack. The bookstore owner in downtown Columbia hated women. Vivian spotted the sign for the bookstore; Crescent Moon Books. She pulled into a parking space a block from the store. Shutting the car door, she checked herself. She wore black jeans and a blue t-shirt with sneakers. In the back pocket of her jeans, a straight razor blade handle stuck up about two inches from the top of the pocket. She could pull the stylist razor from her pocket in less than a second. Stuck in her left shoe, a small folded knife pressed against the heel of her foot. She did not think the weapons would be necessary, but Clyde could be volatile with women he did not trust. She knew this would be a dangerous game.

Vivian pulled the shop door open. Stepping in, she glanced around. Books were stacked in every direction. A mess really. The room mirrored the mind of the shop keeper. They were both ugly and twisted.

Clyde spoke first and said, "I didn't think I would ever see you again." Clyde was pushing fifty years old. The past ten years had not been kind to Clyde. The bushel of black hair had receded back several inches. The green button-down shirt pulled away from the waist. His belly overlapped the belt holding up his khaki pants. His eyes were so brown that they shined like black buttons in the low light. He stood between two stacks of books in the middle of the store.

"Nice to see you too, Clyde," remarked Vivian.

"I can't trust a snake," said Clyde.

"Let's face it. You don't want to see me, but I bring gifts."

"The last time I saw you, you cut me with a razor. I have a scar on my left bicep."

"Well, you got a little handsy."

"If I recall, I just grabbed your butt."

"A girl has to have standards."

"What do you want?"

"Down to business. I need a piece of vellum and a Shamash spell."

"Oh, the Mesopotamian justice God Shamash. You want to kill someone."

"Is that a problem?"

"Hell no, but it will cost you, and I am not talking about money." He leered at Vivian.

"You're old and fat. I would rather sleep with a pig."

Clyde took a step towards Vivian and said, "Be careful, woman."

Vivian stood her ground and said, "I came to trade."

"I don't need your magic potion."

"I think you need more than my magic potion. I have two potions to trade; one for women to forget, and the other to put the lead back into your pencil."

His black eyes stared at Vivian for a moment. She could see the truly evil glare in his eyes. No pity, no remorse, and a hunger to hurt women. His eyes softened like a puppy. Those eyes had fooled too many women.

"What do you want?" asked Clyde.

"A piece of vellum, the spell, and five thousand dollars."

"And why should I not just take it from you, and drag your dead body into the alley?"

"You could try, but my daughter is all grown up now. She would make a formidable enemy."

"The pup. Has she grown?"

"She has become powerful."

"Then why do you need the spell?"

"Let's just say I need to kill a witch."

"A woman, huh? I will give you the spell, the vellum, and three thousand dollars."

"Deal. I would shake on it, but you are a snake in the grass."

Clyde laughed and walked to the back of the store. Vivian felt good. For a moment, she thought Clyde had lost a step. Age can do that to any wicked man, but she knew Clyde to be one of the most wicked men in the South. She would watch him closely. She could hear him open and close a door in the back of the shop. He came back with a sack in his hand.

"You can put the sack on the counter," said Vivian. She saw the small cudgel in his left hand hidden by the sack. "And, you can drop the Billy Club in your left hand."

"Must be getting soft if you saw that even with one eye." Clyde placed the club on a stack of books.

"Back up away from the sack."

Clyde raised his hands, and stepped back several feet. Vivian crossed the distance to the counter. She placed two small jars on the counter. She opened the sack to peer inside. Clyde rushed her. His left fist slugged her in the face. She hit the floor still holding the sack. He grabbed the hair from the back of her head, and twisted it to the side. He raised his meaty fist to pound her face. The straight razor blade scraped his knuckles that held her hair. He howled, and grabbed his injured hand. Blood ran from between his fingers. She had cut all four knuckles on the left hand. Vivian stood up holding the razor blade by the handle. She thought about some choice words to say, but instead ran for the door.

Clyde screamed, "Don't you ever come back here. You hear? I will kill you!"

Vivian ran down the street in the middle of the day. Sunlight flashing on the silver razor blade in her hand. She opened the car door and threw the sack and weapon into the passenger seat. She backed out of the parking spot. She thanked the Goddess that Clyde could not perform magic. She glanced at the seat. A few hundred-dollar bills peeked out of the sack. She laughed at the absurdity of the situation. The potions would perform as discussed with one caveat. His penis would be hard, but for all time. The small sacks of blood that made a man erect would burst if not attended too. The only solution presented to a doctor would be to drain the blood from his erect penis. After that, he would never be erect again.

Chapter Twenty-Eight

The ride to the Grey Witch's home felt like an eternity to Sandra and Ida. Neither of them talked as they drove the backroads to Magenta's home. What could be said? Both of them thought about the true nature of the visit. They wanted to kill someone. Sandra had poured over all the books in her collection on how to reverse the spell created by the Satyr. She could not find anything. The books reiterated that the spell could only be manifested by a witch surviving a sexual encounter with a Satyr. She would then give birth to a Grendel. On a side note, a woman without magic in her blood could survive the brutal sexual encounter with a Satyr, but would not become pregnant. Sandra and Ida wanted to reverse the aging process of the Blood Witch. It was either that or perform a blood magic spell to kill the Blood Witch. Neither of them was willing to use blood magic to kill the witch even if they could find a spell. They felt like reversing the aging process would make the Blood Witch vulnerable and weak; therefore, she would leave them alone and move on.

Sandra parked the car outside of the Grey Witch's home. The small house looked out of place next to the brick buildings in the downtown area. The garden in front of the house still bloomed even in this late part of the summer. Colors sprouted out of every corner. Red, yellow, and green assaulted the senses. Sandra opened the black cast iron gate, and walked up to the door. Ida hung back a couple of steps. Sandra knocked on the door.

After a moment, the door opened. Magenta stood in the door frame. A summer flower dress peeked through her kitchen apron. The apron currently had flour stuck to it. Obviously, she had been baking.

"You surprised me, Sandra. Come in, come in," said Magenta. "Follow me into the kitchen. I am making sweet bread."

Sandra and Ida followed Magenta into the kitchen. The kitchen was in the back of the house. Half of the kitchen was counter space, a stove, and a refrigerator. The cabinets were white and the walls were painted yellow. The other half consisted of a small round table with chairs. Magenta beckoned them to sit at the table. Both of them felt comfortable sitting at the table.

Magenta stood at the counter kneading some baking dough. She said, "I take it things are not going well."

"The Blood Witch and her offspring are not moving on. We, I mean Ida here, cut the monster's hand off, so we think we're in too deep. We do not want to perform blood magic to kill the Blood Witch. So, we thought we could reverse the aging spell, but I can't find anything to help."

"You won't," replied Magenta. "Only a Satyr can reverse the spell. It is a closely guarded secret."

Perplexed, Sandra asked, "So, what do we do?"

"You must find a Satyr. It's easier than you think. Satyrs hang out in bars to pick up drunk women. Usually, the loudest and drunkest man in the bar is a Satyr, but I don't think you want to kidnap some old drunken fool who could be a Satyr. Give me a moment."

Magenta brushed her hands off onto her apron and left the room. A couple of minutes later, she came back into the kitchen carrying a black hand mirror made out of obsidian. Holding the mirror she explained, "This mirror is an Aztec hand mirror. As you can see, it is polished black obsidian. Any reflection in the mirror is true. True in the sense that people have spent years trying to divine their inner soul by looking in the mirror, but it also has the power to see the true nature of a glamoured Faye. Satyrs cannot change their shape, but they do use glamour magic to mask their Faye qualities. This mirror is very old. Hundreds of years old. It has the power to see many things."

"I promise to return the mirror once we are finished," said Sandra.

"No, you will not. The mirror is cursed. When you look into the reflection, you see your time of death. My visage almost matches the reflection in the mirror. I may only have a couple of years left. You do not have to look in the mirror to see if it works, so you can find your Satyr, but you will be greatly tempted to look. I thought about it every day for ten years before I looked in the mirror. That eventuality is the curse. One day, you will look into the mirror and see the age of your death reflected back at you."

"I don't know if I can take it."

"It is your decision only."

Sandra thought about it for a moment. She had to protect her coven, and this was the price. She reached for the mirror. At the handoff, she kept her eyes averted from the reflection of the mirror. This mirror would haunt her for years to come.

"Now," said Magenta, "You must stay for cookies. It will only have to bake a few minutes. Besides, I have not had girl talk in quite some time."

Sandra said, "Ida can tell you a thing or two."

Ida blushed and said, "Yeah, but not the good parts."

The three witches laughed at the joke in the kitchen.

Chapter Twenty-Nine

Again, Jeff found himself staring at the door of the Sheriff's Office. He had completed the training. For once in his life, he felt like he made the right call. The training in Columbia suited him. He made an impression on the trainers for being quite an expert. He figured his father had been covertly training him for this his whole life. He did not mind the subterfuge from his father. In the end, it had paid in dividends.

"Hello Billy," said Jeff as he walked into the police station.

Billy said, "You know there was a time I thought you would never shape up. I'm really glad you're here. Your father is in the back as usual." The phone rang, and Billy picked it up, and said, "Sheriff's Office."

Mike stood beside an empty desk. As Jeff approached, Mike pulled the chair out, and said, "This is yours. Congratulations, son."

Jeff walked up, and offered a hand, and said, "Nice to be here."

Mike pulled him in for a hug. As he released Jeff, he said, "I probably should have done that more often."

Jeff blushed and said, "Maybe."

"Alright, enough chit chat. Your uniform is in the back in the locker room. In a gun safe, you will find your piece. After you're dressed, you speak to Billy about your route today for patrol. Billy is your senior officer. You knock off at seven tonight. Any questions?"

"I don't think so,' said Jeff

"Welcome aboard." Mike turned and headed to his office.

Jeff thought, *"This really happened."*

Several hours later, Jeff pulled his patrol car into Ida's apartment complex. He wanted her impression of the uniform. Of all his friends in town, he wanted to show Ida first. He felt excited about impressing her.

Jeff knocked on the door. It opened, and Ida threw confetti in Jeff's face.

"Surprise," said Ida. She leaned in for a quick kiss. "Sandra baked you a cake."

Jeff walked into the apartment. Balloons drifted around the place with strings attached. A banner hanging from the ceiling said congratulations. Sandra stood in the living room holding a chocolate cake.

Jeff said, "How did you know I would come?"

Sandra replied, "I knew. Now let's eat cake."

As Ida cut the cake into pieces, she said, "Have you found a place yet?"

Jeff said, "Honestly, I haven't found time."

Ducking her head a little Ida said, "I was thinking maybe you should stay here."

"I have a better idea. Old man Johnson is renting a house on the outskirts of town. We should get it together."

Ida clapped her hands with the knife in her hand and said, "I could have a garden."

Jeff hugged her and whispered in her ear, "You can have anything you want. I love you."

Chapter Thirty

An ill wind blew trash into the city gutters. Sheets of rain pushed the trash down the street to collect at low points in the street. Driving slowly in the rain, Vivian and Myra trolled the downtown area in Columbia. City lights pushed against the dark rain. Under street lamps, small circles of light glowed at the top of the poles. The light never reached the ground. The rain cast the city in perpetual darkness. Vivian felt confident no one would see them kidnapping a homeless prostitute. Vivian found what she was looking for in the rain.

A spaghetti of ramps and underpasses where an interstate and a couple of highways converged lay on the outskirts of the city. A maintenance road led to the overpasses. Normally a fence barricaded the road, but the homeless people under the ramps had torn it down. Small tents, lean-tos, and cardboard boxes pushed up against the back of the concrete caves made by the city streets overhead. Vivian stopped the car fifty feet from the edge of the encampment. She tapped the horn twice.

A skinny man wearing dirty board shorts and a light grey sweater ran up to the driver side of the car. The rain plastered his fine blonde hair to his head and bearded face. Holding his hand over his eyes, he stared at the driver side window. Vivian rolled down the window and placed a twenty-dollar bill on the door frame.

The man said, "Rough night to be looking for some fun."

Vivian replied, "We were in a mood."

The young man could see into the car. He could see two women in the front seat. He checked the empty back seat.

"Both of you?" He asked.

"Why not?" answered Vivian. "We've got a cheap motel room for a three-way party."

"They call me Stan the Man," said the homeless prostitute.

"Well, Stan the Man, do you want to party or not? Jump into the backseat."

Stan hesitated for a moment. His usual clientele were usually old gay men. Rarely did a woman ask for his services. Now there were two. Stan looked at them a little closer. The red head was cute, but missing a hand. The dark-haired driver had a cruel scar running down the side of her face with a white glassy eyeball staring back at him. The imperfections actually eased his mind. He figured everyone needed to be loved. He opened the car door and climbed into the backseat.

Leaning forward in the middle of the seat, Stan asked, "Where we headed?"

Vivian replied, "Up the road a bit. Would you like a swig?" She dangled a pint bottle of Roc & Rye from her finger tips.

"Just to take the edge off." Stan grabbed the pint. It was almost empty. "Do you mind if I finish it off and eat the orange peel. The orange peel is the best part."

"No, not at all. We have more where we're going."

Stan turned the bottle up to his lips. Expertly with his tongue, he drew out the orange peel as the liquor poured out of the bottle down his throat. He chewed on the orange peel as his belly slowly warmed up.

"You say you have more of these?"

"Sure," answered Vivian as she slowly backed up the car onto the regular street. "Plenty more."

"I was just starting to have a bad night when you drove up. My tent pole bent. Hey, um, not so fast." Stan felt like the car was speeding down the road. Stan felt the car spin and he promptly fell unconscious.

An hour later, Stan's legs and arms hurt. Feeling a little groggy, Stan shook his head.

"He's coming awake," said Myra.

Stan exclaimed, "What are you bitches doing to me!" His vision cleared enough to see the one room shack. He saw the pot belly stove, the blankets on the floor, and clothes strewn around the room. He tried to stand up, but the ropes tied to his arms and legs held him fast in an old wooden chair. He strained against the bonds. The old wooden chair held, and the ropes dug into his naked flesh. He was naked and bound to a chair. "I don't know what you freaks want, but untie me or so help me god, I am going to hurt you."

Vivian laughed and said, "I don't think so."

"What the fuck is that?" Stan squirmed in the chair. Vivian held a small knife in her hand. "What are you going to do with that?" cried

Stan. He felt a sharp pain in his leg. Vivian had stabbed Stan in the inner thigh. Stan screamed, "What are you doing to me?"

The women laughed at his fear. Stan saw bright red blood drip onto the floor from the wound in his thigh. Vivian came forth again holding a tube and a milk jug. Stan thrashed in his bonds.

"Be still," said Vivian. "This will help."

Not knowing what to do, Stan stopped straining against the rope bonds. He felt a sharp pain as Vivian shoved the tube in the deep cut in his inner thigh. Unbeknownst to him, Vivian had severed the femoral artery in Stan's thigh. The scarlet blood ran down the tube into the milk jug.

"Please stop," moaned Stan. "I won't say a thing."

"No, you won't Stan," said Vivian patting him on the shoulder. "No, you won't."

Stan watched the blood filter down the tube into the milk jug. He wondered how much blood in the human body would fill a milk jug. As his heart slowed from the loss of blood, Stan watched the blood slowly fill the milk jug. He wanted to fight, but he could not feel anything. His arms, legs, and chest seemed to be going numb. He wanted to cry for help, but could not draw enough breath into his lungs.

"Momma," cried out Stan right before he died in that shitty shack.

Chapter Thirty-One

Sandra drove into the parking lot of a hook up club. A large square building sat in a parking lot the size of a football field. No one knew the name of the club. On the outside, high in the sky, a large yellow sign flashed the word Dance. The party never started before late in the night. This was the last-ditch effort of drunk people filtering in from other bars across the city of Columbia. Cheap beer flowed, and women moved on the dance floor.

Sandra sat in the driver's seat. Her hands shook ever so slightly. She had made a plan, and now she had to see it through. Ida had argued that going alone was a stupid idea, but to trap a predator like a Satyr you had to look wounded and like easy prey. Sandra checked her make-up in the rear-view mirror. The mascara on her eyes ran in the corners like she had been crying. The makeup had been applied thick on her face. She wore a cardboard, gold tierra with BIRTHDAY written in bold letters across the center. She adjusted her breasts in the bra, making them look perky. A tiny black skirt that barely covered her ass rode up high on her thighs as she sat in the car seat. She checked the parking lot one more time. More than half full, the place should be rocking.

Sandra walked across the parking lot. In two days, the moon would be full. Right now, the light from the moon lit up the parking lot. She weaved her way through the parked cars to the entrance. A door man stopped her at the black door with one small light shining down from a weak bulb high above his head.

"I.D.," he said.

"This is my I.D.," said Sandra pointing to the birthday crown.

The man did not speak a word and held out his hand.

"Ok, ok," said Sandra. "Gimme a minute." She dug into the small clutch bag and produced her driver's license.

"Today is not your birthday," said the doorman while checking her license.

"It's everybody's birthday," said Sandra.

"Yeah, yeah," said the doorman. He reached behind him and opened the door.

Sandra grabbed her license and went through the door. As she walked into the club, she smelled stale beer and stale cigarette smoke. She had to stop for a moment to let her eyes adjust to the murky light. Speakers dotted the walls spilling out loud music. In the center of tables and chairs a dance floor with a railing running around its edge was full of dancing people. The source of most of the light in the bar came from the bartender station against one wall. Three bartenders were working the length of a mahogany wooden bar. The noise and lack of light made Sandra nervous. How was she going to find a Satyr in this chaos?

Sandra slowly made her way to the bar. Acting drunk, she walked like she was navigating an ice patch. She found a stool and plopped down on it heavily. She held out a five-dollar bill. A bartender plucked it from her hand and yelled, "What do you want?"

She yelled back, "Vodka martini."

He moved behind the bar for a moment, then dropped a glass in front of Sandra. She had no idea how much the drink cost. She assumed the five-dollar bill covered the drink. She spun around on the bar stool and played with the Aztec mirror. Pretending to apply lip stick using the mirror, she angled the mirror to pass over the crowd. In the middle of the dance floor a Satyr stomped his feet in time with the music. Sandra quickly put the mirror back in her clutch bag.

Sandra tipped the glass spilling vodka on her shirt. Half empty, she downed the remaining portion of clear vodka. After drinking, she actually ran for the dance floor. Holding her arms above her head, Sandra gyrated her hips. The Satyr danced his way through the crowd and put his hands on her hips. Standing six feet tall, the Satyr looked human. Long brown chestnut hair cascaded down his back. His eyes were emerald green. He wore a button-down white shirt, the buttons opened to his belly. Black jeans and cowboy boots completed the ensemble. Laughing, Sandra pushed her hips against his as they danced.

The song ended. Sandra grabbed his belt buckle and planted a kiss full on the mouth. She then led him off the stage and headed for the door. She pulled him out of the club.

Standing by a pick-up truck, she French kissed the Satyr. After a moment, she leaned into his embrace and whispered into his ear, "I have a room."

"My car or yours?" replied the Satyr.

"Mine, and it is not far away. Do you mind driving? I think I am a little drunk."

"No problem. Which one is yours?"

"The little bug over there," said Sandra, pointing to her car.

The VW Bug pulled out of the parking lot headed away from Columbia. Sandra would only laugh and point out each turn for the Satyr. The Bug wound its way out of the city limits. On a dark road, lights flashed, and a siren wailed.

"Shit," said the Satyr. "Are you holding?"

"No," answered Sandra. "Are you drunk?"

"I can handle it."

The Satyr pulled the car over on a desolate stretch of road. Woods were on both sides of the road. He turned off the motor and the head lights. He rolled down the window and put his hands at ten and two on the steering wheel.

The officer flashed a light in the Satyr's face and demanded, "Get out of the car."

"Why, officer? I was doing the speed limit," said the Satyr.

"Get out of the car, now," said the officer.

The Satyr opened the door and stepped out onto the easement next to the car. The officer spun him and pinned him against the side of the car. The officer handcuffed the Satyr and pushed him down into a sitting position on the road against the car.

"What the fuck did I do wrong?" admonished the Satyr.

Jeff replied, "Ask the woman."

Sandra came around the back of the car and said, "You can lose the glamour spell."

"What?" asked the Satyr.

"I'm not kidding," said Sandra.

"I need to keep an eye on the road," replied Jeff. He walked a couple feet away from the Satyr and Sandra, keeping an eye on both the Satyr and the road.

The Satyr asked, "What do you want?"

Sandra replied, "I need a counter spell to the longevity spell."

The Satyr laughed and asked, "And why would I give you that?"

"I could cut your balls off and feed them to you," said Sandra.

"You're bluffing. You may have a cop in your pocket, but you smell like a Nature Witch. You are not going to harm me."

"Just give me the counter spell," said Sandra.

"No," replied the Satyr. "Now let me go."

Sandra walked over to Jeff and whispered, "What do we do now? He called my bluff."

Jeff replied, "I don't know anything about Satyrs, but I don't think he would like to be locked up."

Jeff turned and said, "How about a couple of days in the slammer."

"On what charges?" asked the Satyr.

"Drunk and disorderly," answered Jeff.

The Satyr squirmed a little. "I can't go to jail."

"Why not?" asked Jeff.

"Please, listen. I can only keep the glamour spell going for a couple of hours."

"So, then you become a monster in a cage," said Jeff.

"What do you want from me?"

Sandra replied, "I need the counter spell."

The Satyr stirred again. "You're asking a lot. It's kind of a trade secret."

Sandra replied, "I wouldn't ask if it were not life and death. A Blood Witch is killing my coven."

"I need my hands free," said the Satyr.

Jeff said, "Ok, but don't stand up." Jeff leaned over and undid the cuffs.

The Satyr rubbed his wrists. He glared at them both for a moment and then transformed into his natural self. The Satyr looked half human and half goat. The top half consisted of antlers on his head, a shaggy main almost covering his face, and a bare, naked chest. The lower half looked like a goat with hairy legs and hooves.

The Satyr replied, "You do not know how lucky you are. I only molt every ten years, but you timed it right and my antlers are a little brittle." The Satyr reached up and broke off a small piece of the antler. "You have to grind this up, and the Blood Witch must inhale the dust."

Sandra replied, "That's it?"

The Satyr said, "That's it. My antlers are magical in nature. We keep that a secret. I don't want my head cut off for someone's spell."

Sandra replied, "I will keep it a secret until the day I die."

Jeff said, "And me."

The Satyr stood up on its hind legs. It shook itself and bound across the road into the woods.

Chapter Thirty-Two

The full moon rose above the trees of the shack. Being this far from the city lights, the moon cast an eerie glow with moving shadows in the woods. Flickers of candle-light shown through the cracks in the wood of the shack. Crystal clear skies above the shack showed stars that seemed embedded in a tapestry of black.

The Blood Witch had prepared the dirty cabin for the spell. Everything had been pushed to the walls of the shack creating a space in the middle of the floor. Three candles, forming a triangle, burned in the middle of the clearing. Holding the milk jug of blood, Vivian poured the blood on the floorboards in the shape of a pentagram while murmuring an incantation. Myra stood in a corner. Myra's eyes were bright and her face was ecstatic. Dark forces were being conjured here.

Vivian threw the empty milk jug into a corner. Holding the piece of vellum above her head, she danced around the perimeter of the pentagram. Her naked body swayed back and forth, and the keloid scars on her arms and legs glowed a sickening red in the candle-light. The dance was meant to be a tribute to the dark justice god Shamash. Written in Myra's blood on the vellum, Ida's name started to glow yellow. After one final spin and shout of tribute, Vivian flung the vellum into the center of the pentagram. The spell had been cast.

When the vellum touched the floor, it burst into a green ball of flame. As the flame slowly rotated on the floor, an amniotic sack of viscous liquid appeared out of the flame. The size of a basketball, the sack pulsed on the floor. Something hideous pushed insect like arms against the sides of the membrane. The gelatinous sack burst, and an insect created in hell scuttled around the inside of the pentagram. A cross between a spider and a cockroach, and as large as a basketball, the thing pushed against the boundaries of the pentagram center. After a minute, the thing spun a cocoon in the middle of the pentagram. The cocoon hung in thin air a few feet off the boards. It climbed up into the cocoon. Gathering on the bottom of the rotating cocoon, a viscous blue liquid dripped onto the floor. The thing started to spin faster. The blood pentagram levitated off the floor to the height of the cocoon. The cocoon burst, and blue viscous liquid and the spidery web flung debris against the walls of the shack. The bloody pentagram rotated twice in the air, and then spattered down upon the floor. In the center of the room, a black shadow levitated off the boards. The size of a newborn baby, the shadow's eyes, as red as smoldering charcoal, pierced the heart of Myra. The shadow moved for the door. It had judged the venomous revenge in Myra's heart, and found Myra's heart wanting justice for her lost hand.

***

Sandra came down the stairs in her shop to get the latest magazine. Light from the large windows cast shadows in the shop. Out of the corner of her eye, she saw something move. Ever so slightly, a shadow drifted across the floor. Before she could react, two flames for eyes pierced her soul. The flames blinked out, and the shadow started for the stairs. Sandra turned and ran up the stair case.

She screamed, "Ida!"

At the top of the stairs, she grabbed Ida's arm leading her to the bathroom. She turned on the cold and hot tap. She plugged the bathtub as the water ran.

Sandra said, "Listen carefully. Get in the tub."

Ida balked and asked, "What's going on?"

"Get in the damn tub, and I will tell you later." Sandra ran from the bathroom. Running to her bedroom closet, Sandra pulled everything off the top shelf. Clothes, boxes, and a Ouija board fell on the floor. Sandra grabbed the Ouija board. Running out of the room, she grabbed a pair of scissors off her dresser. At the top of the stairs, the shadow loomed. Sandra backed up into the bathroom keeping an eye on the shadow.

Ida asked harshly, "What's going on?"

"There's a demon in the house, and I think it is coming for you," answered Sandra.

Sounding scared, Ida asked, "What do I do?"

"When it comes into the bathroom, you must completely submerge yourself in the water. Nothing must poke out. Try to stay under the water as long as you can." Sandra grabbed Ida's hand and cut Ida's palm with the scissor blade. Sandra then pressed Ida's bloody palm against the Ouija board. She dropped the board in front of the tub, and put her back against the wall.

The shadow crept into the room. The two fiery eyes flared again. Instead of going out, the demon locked onto Ida's heart. It drifted towards the tub.

"Now," screamed Sandra.

Ida ducked her body into the water. Her eyes wide, she saw the shadow at the edge of the tub. The demon lingered there. Thirty seconds passed, still the demon hovered. A minute passed, and Ida felt her lungs cramp. Ida expelled some air into the water. Small bubbles percolated on top of the water in the tub. She wanted to breath. She started crying, and water swept her tears from her face. She felt doomed. She had to come up for air. The shadow's eyes flashed once, then it slowly sank below the lip of the outside of the tub. Ida gave it one more second, then raised her head to gasp for air.

Sucking in air, Ida managed to ask, "Where is it?"

Sandra came over and sat on the edge of the tub. She said, "In the Ouija board."

Still crying, Ida asked, "Forever?"

"Yes, dear."

"How?"

Sandra pulled Ida to her. She cradled Ida's head against her bosom, and said, "There is no water on the astral plane. The demon could not find you, so it went for your blood. It trapped itself in the Ouija board."

"What do we do now?"

Sandra cradled Ida's face in her hands and said, "We kill the bitches."

Chapter Thirty-Three

Sandra and Ida prepared for war. First, they gathered instruments of death. Ida grabbed the cursed knife. The knife seemed to glow ever so slightly. An implement of death, the knife yearned for the target it had been created for. Sandra grabbed two vials of the Satyr's antler. Ground down to a fine dust, the magic from the antler waited for a victim.

Ida asked, "How do we dress for something like this?"

Sandra replied, "I guess we want something loose, so we can move quickly. Also, something to protect ourselves."

"Blue jean suit?"

"Yeah, I see what you're saying. We wear blue jeans and a blue jean jacket. The material should afford us some protection, and we can easily move in them. We also need heavy boots for weapons."

Ida stripped out of her clothes down to her underwear. Out of her overnight bag, she grabbed a pair of blue jeans and pulled them up her thighs. She pulled a loose-fitting brown t-shirt out, and covered the t-shirt with a blue jean jacket. She reached for her hiking boots and pulled them on. She double knotted the laces to make them secure. She checked herself in the mirror. She felt a little silly wearing something like a man's suit, but it was comfortable.

Sandra came out of the bathroom dressed exactly like Ida. Both girls wore a blue jean suit, but unlike Ida, Sandra carried the Ouija board carefully in her hands. Sandra placed it on the coffee table in her small living room.

"What are you doing with that?" asked Ida.

"It is going to give us the location of the Blood Witch," answered Sandra. Holding the planchet, Sandra asked, "Where is the Blood Witch that summoned you?"

Slowly the planchet moved and spelled out "slave shack". After the spelling, the board vibrated violently. Sandra quickly removed her hands and said, "I think it's pissed."

"Where are we going to find a slave shack?"

Sandra slowly stuffed the Ouija board under the couch and replied, "There is only one slave shack near here. It is on an old plantation. I should have known they were there. It's isolated, but near the town. Are you ready for this?"

"They have tried to kill me on several occasions. I think it's payback time," said Ida, wielding the knife in one hand and holding the vial in the other hand.

"I'm with you,' said Sandra. "Let's go."

As both of them walked out of the backdoor to Sandra's shop, Ida stopped and grabbed a metal lid off a trash can. She shook it a couple of times. It felt right.

Sandra asked, "What are you going to do with that?"

"I thought it would make a good shield. The damn monster's claws are sharp."

"Great idea, get in the car."

Sandra drove her beetle out of town. The summer air pushed hot air into the car. The full moon cast shadows from trees onto the blacktop of the road outside of town. Neither girl spoke. Both of them felt grim resignation. They were going to kill two monsters, or be killed trying to rid the world of two evil beings.

Sandra stopped the car a half mile from the shack. Standing in front of the car, they checked their weapons.

Ida asked, "Do we have a plan?"

"Lucky for us, I think we will take them by surprise. You go for the Grendel, and I will take the Blood Witch."

As they walked down the dirt road, the woods were alive with wildlife. Crickets were chirping. Things rustled the leaves. The sway of the trees in the summer wind cast shadows from the full moon onto the dirt road. Both of them were scared shitless.

As they approached the shack, they could hear the two things laughing. Light cascaded out of the front door. The trunk of the car was open. They were going to make their escape tonight. Clothes and sundry things were spilling out of the trunk of the blue Buick.

"I'll go first," whispered Ida.

Sandra just nodded assent.

Taking a deep breath, Ida rushed the door. At the entrance, Ida tripped over the dead body of the prostitute. She stumbled into a nightmare. Blood soaked the floor. The Blood Witch and the Grendel had been cavorting in the blood. Both naked, grime and blood covered their naked bodies. Both of them were in the back of the room. Both of them were laughing at the horror written on Ida's face.

Vivian said, "You do know how to make an entrance."

Ida felt a pain of shock after glancing around the room and said, "I never thought of anything being evil until now."

Vivian walked over to the stove and picked up the machete, saying, "I have seen evil. Evil is a construct. I don't consider myself evil in the world of men."

Sandra stepped into the doorway and said, "I think you are buying time."

Vivian said, "Time is not relevant when you're over a hundred years old. And yes, I was buying time. Time to find out who the players are. Is that lovely young man here as well?"

Ida answered, "No."

Vivian tested the blade of the machete on her finger and said, "That was a mistake. You might have survived this."

Myra screamed and rushed forward with a butcher's knife. Ida took the blow on the makeshift shield. The metal bent around her forearm from the mighty blow, but Ida punched up with her knife under the shield and stabbed Myra in the stomach. Myra stumbled back holding her stomach with her hands.

No blood exited the wound in Myra's stomach. Dark, venomous smoke poured from a gaping hole. The hole widened, and more smoke spewed forth. The smoke seemed to coalesce around Myra. Myra fell to her knees. The smoke enveloped her. Myra evaporated on the floor.

Vivian screamed, "I won't be so easy, bitch!" Vivian howled and levitated off the floor. She cut her palm with the machete and then slung the blood from the cut, hitting both their faces with warm blood. Spreading her arms and legs wide, her hair swirled around her head. Her one good eye rolled into the back of her head. She started the chant, "I curse you."

Sandra grabbed Ida and yelled, "Get out!"

Ida ran for the door. She wiped the blood off her face with her hands. She turned at the doorframe and stared at both witches. Red flames flickered around the Blood Witch's body. Vivian seemed to be chanting in Greek. Things in the room burst into flames. Clothes, furniture, and other items had flames licking from them.

Sandra grabbed the pendent she wore around her neck for good luck. She started her own enchantment. A force field the size of a door appeared in front of Sandra. It pushed against the flames being emitted by the Blood Witch. Sandra took a step closer. The shield held, but flames licked around the edges. Sandra took another step. The flames were hot. Sandra's clothes started to smoke. Sandra's head was only a couple feet from the Blood Witch's knees. The walls of the shack caught fire. In moments, the roof would collapse. Sandra broke the magical vial in her hand, and threw the contents of the vial at the Blood Witch's head. Sandra did not wait to see the effect of the powder on the Blood Witch. Instead, she hurriedly backed her way out of the room.

Inhaling deeply for the last line of the curse, Vivian felt the dust enter her mouth. Still levitating in the middle of the floor, she screamed her last breath. She dropped to the floor of the shack. Ninety years of hard abuse rushed into her limbs. Her hair grew three feet. Her skin wrinkled like a raisin. Her limbs contorted into a fetal position. The angry flames in the shack consumed her.

Sandra backed out of the door from the inferno of flames. At the door frame, Ida grabbed her from behind and pulled her clear of the burning shack. Coughing up smoke from her tortured lungs, Sandra watched the building burn.

A patrol car skidded to a halt a few yards from the girls. Jeff ran up to the girls as the shanty collapsed on itself. Ida was on the ground holding Sandra in her arms. Both of them were crying from immense relief.

Jeff shouted above the roar of the fire, "Are you alright?"

Ida ran into Jeff's arms, crying. She squeezed him with all her strength.

Sandra sat up and said, "Tell your father, the bodies in the shack were the murderers."

"I don't know if he will believe me," said Jeff.

"Just tell him I said so," said Sandra.

All three of them could hear a fire engine in the distance. All three of them watched the shack burn. They were finally safe from the denizens of evil.

Chapter Thirty-Four

Sandra sat on the stool behind the store counter. She had just stripped her nails of the blue fingernail polish. She imagined blood in the crevices of the blue polish. She hoped that the light pink nail polish would cover the imaginary blood on her hands. She knew killing them was the right thing to do, but it had taken a toll on her heart. The bell on the door clanged and Sandra stood to attention when Mike walked into the store.

Sandra asked, "You're not in uniform?"

Mike answered, "This is a friendly visit. I have a couple of questions."

"Shoot."

"Is it over?"

Sandra sat back down on the stool and replied, "Yes, it is over. Both the murderers were in the shack. The Grendel evaporated into smoke which left the original murderer."

"We found two bodies. One male and one female."

"I don't know who the male victim was, but that was the last murder."

"What was she?"

"A witch. A terrible witch. Something nightmares are made of. Did you convince the authorities that she was the murderer?"

"Yeah, and don't think I didn't know about the run on the license plate. I convinced the state police that the vehicle had been spotted at all the crime scenes. They bought it."

"Thank the goddess for that."

"On a different note, what is this girl Ida all about?"

Sandra laughed and said, "She will keep him on his toes."

"They're moving in together. Jeff has broken a lot of hearts in his time, but I have never seen him like this. If you say she's okay then she's good in my book. Besides, they do seem to be happy."

"That's all you can wish for."

"Being in love is a gift. Try and stay out of trouble."

Sandra saluted Mike and said, "Yes sir."

As Mike walked out of the store, Sandra imagined his step was more chipper. Sandra looked at her fingernails and imagined them clean from blood. Her heart blossomed. Everyone in the town and the witches in her coven were safe. That was just what she wanted.

Made in the USA
Middletown, DE
28 February 2022